Bar 10 Gunsmoke

As always, tough Bar 10 rancher Gene Adams responded to an urgent plea for help. With no thought to their own safety, Adams, Johnny Puma and Tomahawk headed into Mexico to help their old friend Don Miguel García.

But all was not as it appeared. Unknown to Adams and his pals, they were walking into a carefully planned trap laid by the infamous outlaw known only as Lucifer. No sooner had the three Bar 10 riders arrived at García's ranch, than Johnny was cut down in a hail of bullets.

Vowing vengeance, Adams and Tomahawk thunder straight into action to take on Lucifer and his gang. But will they survive the outlaws' hot lead?

Bar 10 Gunsmoke

Boyd Cassidy

A Black Horse Western

ROBERT HALE · LONDON

© Boyd Cassidy 2005
First published in Great Britain 2005

ISBN 0 7090 7710 6

Robert Hale Limited
Clerkenwell House
Clerkenwell Green
London EC1R 0HT

Typeset by
Derek Doyle & Associates, Shaw Heath.
Printed and bound in Great Britain by
Antony Rowe Limited, Wiltshire

*Dedicated with heartfelt thanks to my friend
and fellow ex-salty dog, television and film star,
Clint 'Cheyenne' Walker and his lovely wife Susan*

PROLOGUE

Blood-red shafts of crimson stretched out across the late-afternoon sky above the parched land. It was as if the heavens were desperately trying to warn the mere mortals below of what was about to occur. The dozen horsemen drove their lathered-up mounts across the sun-drenched terrain towards the distant line of trees. A fast-flowing river made its presence known as its white-water rapids cut through the rocky landscape, sending plumes of spray up into the sky. With the last rays of the dying sun dancing off the ceaselessly moving water vapour, a rainbow arched above the trees as if warning what was awaiting them once they rode into range of the outlaws' Winchesters.

Gene Adams dragged his reins up to his chest and raised his right hand to signal his fellow riders to follow suit. Dust drifted up off the hoofs of the exhausted mounts as they all stopped beside the Bar 10 rancher. Adams stood in his stirrups and glared out into the heat haze before them. There was concern carved into his handsome rugged features.

'What do you see, Señor Gene?' Colonel Luis García asked as he urged his mount closer to the tall chestnut mare. 'Do you see Lucifer and his men?'

Adams lowered himself back on to his saddle and tilted his head slightly. His blue eyes stared at his friend and then the rest of the riders beside them. They were a mixture of Mexican soldiers and his own Bar 10 cowboys. Each of then proudly wore the gleaming federal government special agent's stars on their chests. Stars that bore witness to the fact that they had been specially chosen by both the Mexican and Texan government to hunt down and capture the most dangerous gang of outlaws ever to have raided on both sides of the long border. A gang that had shown their victims no mercy.

'Yep, I see them.' Gene Adams's low voice drawled as he saw the sunlight trace along the barrels of the outlaws' rifles.

Rip Calloway drew his horse level with his boss and shaded his eyes from the blinding sun that danced off the white-water spray a quarter-mile ahead of them.

'How many of them do you reckon there are, Gene?' the young cowboy asked.

'Too many, Rip,' Adams snapped. 'Way too many, son.'

Colonel García carefully checked his revolver and then swallowed hard.

'Do you think that we will be able to capture them all, Señor Gene?'

Adams raised an eyebrow and then grinned.

'Nope. I figure we've got a fight on our hands, Luis.' The answer was honest. The Texas rancher knew that there was far more possibility of their being killed than being able to get the drop on Lucifer and his gang of deadly followers. 'They ain't gonna give up easy when all they've got to look forward to is a hangman's noose. You better make sure that every one of them guns is loaded and ready for action. Fill your pockets with bullets now 'coz there might not be any time to pluck them out of your gunbelts once the shooting starts.'

Calloway turned and faced the rest of the riders. Every face was staring at the broad-shouldered Adams. They had followed him a long way to this spot and knew that they might never leave this place alive if they did not heed Adams's every command. For Gene Adams was a living legend in the West. A man who had been around long before any of them were born, and had survived every thing that this harsh land had thrown at him.

If there was one man who could defeat Lucifer, it was the rancher with the white hair and tanned face.

'You heard Gene. Check them hoglegs and fill your pockets with bullets, boys,' Calloway

9

instructed the cowboys.

García repeated the order to his own men in Spanish.

Gene Adams lifted his canteen up, unscrewed the stopper and raised it to his dry lips. He sipped at the water thoughtfully.

'Do you think that they are waiting to ambush us?' García asked the question although he already knew the answer.

'Yep, Luis! They're waiting, OK.' Adams returned his canteen to the saddle horn, then studied the terrain before them. Few trees ventured far away from the damp soil close to the fast-moving rapids. There were a few large, smooth boulders scattered across the flat sand which marked the distance between the outlaws and the riders. Long black shadows snaked their way over the almost white sand as the sun sank ever lower in the cloudless sky.

'If they are waiting with their rifles they will be able to pick us off one by one as we ride at them,' the colonel muttered as he too contemplated the land between themselves and the deadly killers they sought.

'I already figured that, Luis!' Adams said rubbing his chin with his gloved fingers. 'We have to figure out how we get from here to there without getting picked off. I ain't partial to being in no turkey shoot.'

'It'll be dark soon, Gene,' Calloway noted, pointing at the red orb to their left. 'We ought to wait until sunset and try to get the drop on them in the dark.'

Adams glanced at the features of the cowboy. He smiled and then pointed behind them at the sky. A large moon had already started to cast its eerie light across the land.

'I don't think we'll be able to use darkness to sneak up on them, not with that darn moon up there. It'll be almost as light as day, even after sundown.'

The young cowboy felt a chill overwhelm him.

It was fear.

'Then what we gonna do, Gene?'

Adams turned his reins and aimed his horse's head to their left. He pointed a finger at the line of trees that fringed the horizon.

'We head there! That's a couple of miles up river from where Lucifer and his scum are holed up.'

'And then we make our way down river?' García asked.

'Yep!' Adams nodded. 'It'll take hours, but the trees that line the riverbank will give us cover.'

García leaned across the distance between them.

'But they'll see us and know what we are doing, Señor Gene. They will not remain in the same place. Lucifer is too clever to be tricked that easily.'

Adams gritted his teeth.

'Lucifer's smart OK, but he ain't gonna figure out what we're doing 'cos we're leaving half our men here. They'll start to fire at the outlaws whilst you, me and the rest of the boys make a wide circle around to them trees.'

'Will it work?'

Gene Adams sighed heavily.

'Ask me that after the gunsmoke clears, Luis!'

The six riders had carefully retraced their tracks until they were convinced that Lucifer and his gang could no longer see them from their hiding-place near the river. Then they had heard Rip and the rest of their men opening up with their Winchesters, as Adams had ordered.

Darkness had spread across the remote land long before the half-dozen horsemen eventually reached the line of trees that edged the bank of the river. A tree-line that went all the way along the riverbank to the rapids.

Adams gently encouraged his chestnut mare down through the trees toward the fast-flowing water with the five riders close behind his mount's tail.

The tall handsome horse led the way slowly down river as the sound of the six riders' comrades' rifles continued to fire across the flat range in the distance.

'C'mon!' Adams growled. He jabbed his spurs and allowed his mare its head.

For more than ten eternal minutes, the half dozen skilled horsemen galloped over the muddy ground beside the raging river until the keen-eyed Adams spotted the moonlight glancing off the rifle barrels of their prey.

Then the entire area lit up as Lucifer and his outlaws opened up with their weaponry. Deadly bullets blasted into the group of riders, sending two men to Adams's right tumbling into the ice-cold water.

Without a sound the rancher leapt from his saddle and hauled his two golden Colts from their hand-tooled holsters. He started to return fire as he watched the three remaining riders desperately dismount and seek cover.

Only when satisfied that they had found the safety of large trees and boulders did the Bar 10 rancher throw himself down on to his belly behind a clump of rocks next to the water's edge.

Even though he was half in the icy water, Adams continued firing at the plumes of gunsmoke which spewed from the barrels of the outlaw Winchesters until something touched his leg.

He turned his head and focused his eyes on the body of the Mexican as it floated past him. The star on the dead man's chest flashed, then the body disappeared beneath the foaming white water.

'This ain't good, Gene!' The familiar voice of Happy Summers echoed out across the distance between them as bullets continued to keep them pinned down.

'Just suck in that belly of yours and keep shoot-ing, boy!' Adams replied as he emptied the spent shells from his guns and then thoughtfully reloaded his weapons.

'I think we have killed some of them, Señor Gene!' García yelled from behind the broad trunk of a tree which was being torn to shreds by the outlaws' bullets.

'Don't count no chickens yet, Luis!' Adams said. He snapped both gun chambers with expert flicks of his wrists, hauled back the hammers and then leaned out over the water to get a better view of their attackers. They were well dug in and barely visible, but Adams only required the slightest hint of a target to be able to hit it.

The three men a few yards away from the rancher continued to fan their gun hammers at the outlaws, but Adams knew that they were outgunned.

None of the survivors of Adam's men had managed to get their Winchesters from their saddle scabbards when they had thrown themselves from the lathered-up horses. Lucifer's men had the advantage of having had time to plan their defence. They had ensured that they had the best cover and all their vast arsenal of weaponry at their fingertips. The outlaws' long rifles were keeping Adams and his men exactly where they wanted them.

Gene Adams rested his spine against the cold rocks and stared at the scene about them. It was grim. The bandits' bullets were blazing all around them, taking chunks out of the boulders and tree-trunks that he and his men were hiding behind. It seemed as if they had managed to do the one thing that Adams had wanted to avoid.

They had ridden into the trap Lucifer had set for them.

The rancher screwed up his eyes and gritted his teeth as more bullets carved the rocks at his back and showered him with even more fine dust.

Adams knew that he had to do something if he and his trusting followers were going to get the better of his foes. If he did nothing, he knew that eventually the outlaws would fan out and close in on them.

'What's wrong, Gene?' Happy shouted out as he watched the brooding rancher staring back along the trail.

Adams glanced at the troubled cowboy and waved one of his golden guns before holstering both of the gleaming Colts.

'Reckon you boys can give me a little cover, Happy?'

The well-rounded cowboy hastily reloaded his own gun as he watched the rancher removing his heavy top coat and hat and place them on the muddy ground.

'What you thinking of doin', Gene?'

'Just give me cover! OK?' Adams pulled his gloves over his hands until he could see his finger-nails through the black kid leather.

The three men did as Adams had requested and started to fire their handguns blindly at the outlaws as they watched in a mixture of horror and awe as the Bar 10 rancher began to make his way

15

along the river-bank on all fours.

Gene Adams kept ducking down as the odd stray bullet skimmed over his crouching figure. Yet he did not hesitate for even a mere beat of his pounding heart. He kept on heading towards the six terrified horses which had fled as soon as their masters had dropped off their saddles.

'Where is Señor Gene going?' asked the colonel as he kept firing his guns. 'Could he be running away from this battle?'

Happy spat and looked around the tree-trunk at the confused Mexican officer.

'You joshin', Colonel? Gene got something up his sleeve. I reckon them outlaws are in for one big surprise!'

Adams glanced back over his shoulder at the lethal venom which was still blasting at his three comrades. He inhaled deeply and then looked up at his nervous chestnut mare as she in turn continued to stare at the incessant gunfire.

'Easy, girl!' Adams soothed as he reached up to the loose reins of the skittish horse. 'Easy now. Ain't none of them bullets gonna hurt ya.'

Slowly the rancher pulled himself up until he was standing beside his trusting mount. He stroked her neck as his eyes narrowed and kept watching the battle a mere hundred yards downriver. He pulled the coiled cutting-rope from the saddle horn and then dragged out his Winchester.

'You stay here, girl. Even them egg-suckers couldn't miss a target as big as you.'

The horse watched as her master looped the rope over his shoulder and then made his way back to the edge of the fast-flowing river. Adams kept low and continued heading back to where he had left his coat and hat. Only when he was a few yards away from the rocks did a volley of bullets come anywhere near him.

Adams felt the impact of the rifle bullets as they tore through his shirt and burned the flesh off his left shoulder.

'Damn!' Adams snarled angrily as he fell back behind the rocks again. 'Them varmints winged me!'

Adams looked across at García.

'You any good with a carbine, Luis?' Adams asked above the sound of the rifle fire.

'*Sí, amigo!*' the colonel answered.

'Then have this one.' Gene Adams tossed the Winchester with all his strength and watched as his friend caught it cleanly.

Ignoring the bullets which still carved chunks out of the rocks behind him, Adams carefully untied the buckles holding his leather batwing chaps. He pulled them free of his legs and then dropped them down between his legs. The rancher was working feverishly to the confusion of his three onlookers. He had found his penknife, drawn it from his vest pocket and unfolded its razor-sharp blade. He sliced through the well-worn leather of one of the chaps and made a square. He then repeated the action and started to wrap his

17

golden guns in the water-repellent leather. He then plucked his ten-gallon hat up off the damp ground and cut its drawstring into two equal lengths.

Adams speedily tied the leather around the wrapped guns with the drawstrings. Then he unbuttoned his shirt. His gloved fingers slid both weapons into his shirt.

'Why have you got the rope, Señor Gene?' García's voice rang out as he saw the rancher get back on to his knees. 'Is it not too early to hang these men? We have to stop getting killed first. *Sí, amigo?*'

Adams eyes glanced at the army officer. A man who was as good as any he had ever encountered during his long life.

'Just shoot some of them varmints with that Winchester, Luis!' the rancher winked through the smoke. 'Now you got the range to match any of them.'

The Mexican officer cranked the mechanism of the rifle and then aimed up to where Lucifer and the rest of the outlaws were dug in. His first bullet found its target and sent an outlaw flying backward.

'That's more like it, Luis!' Adams shouted as he watched the colonel repeat his action with equal deadliness. Then the rancher returned his full attention to the coiled rope. Slowly he started to unwind it until he was satisfied with its length. He made a lasso and looped it over the stoutest of the boulders beside him and tightened the rope.

Adams then found the other end of the rope and tied it around his chest under his armpits. He adjusted the carefully wrapped guns inside his shirt and licked his dry lips.

His blue eyes narrowed and stared at the raging white water beside him. There was no way that Lucifer or any of his cohorts would expect anyone, let alone a man of Adams's age, to attempt what the rancher was about to do.

To the amazement of his three comrades, the rancher rolled off the muddy bank and disappeared into the icy-cold water. He disappeared beneath the white foam.

Happy Summers stretched up to his full height against the trunk of the tree and watched as the slack rope slithered into the river like a viper.

'What in tarnation is going on?' Happy gasped as his fingers fumbled shells into the red-hot chambers of his Colt.

'Easy, *amigo*. I think Señor Gene has gone fishing!' García said. He cranked the Winchester again and continued firing at the distant outlaws.

The words of the Mexican officer were a lot closer to the truth than he might have imagined.

Adams had never been much of a swimmer, but with the long cutting-rope tied firmly around his chest, he knew that all he had to do was hold his breath long enough until he was washed downriver. He felt the jagged rocks beneath the surface of the white water cutting into the flesh of his shoulders and back as he continued to be washed helplessly along.

It had been a rough guess as to how far down-river Lucifer and his gang were in relation to the length of the long rope, but Gene Adams had always managed to rely on his luck.

Once again, she was kind to him.

The rancher felt the rope tighten around him as his head broke through the surface water. He grabbed on to its wet length, fought against the incredible current and shook his head until his eyes cleared.

The power of the relentless water pounded him like a hundred irate longhorn steers, yet Adams clung on to the slippery rope. He had done what he had hoped he would do. He had managed to get behind the gang.

The moonlight illuminated the backs of the outlaws, twenty feet away. It took every ounce of his dwindling strength to fight his way back towards the bank of the angry river. He dug his boot-heels into the rough rocks below him and managed to get closer to the elusive riverbank.

Inch by inch Adams forced himself nearer to the rocks and river weed. He knew that if any of the outlaws were to look over their shoulders, he was done for. Yet the colonel and the two remaining cowboys were managing to keep them occupied.

Adams reached out with his left hand and grabbed hold of a branch. He used its suppleness to pull himself clear of the water and drop down on the black rocks. Yet the river was not finished with the Bar 10 rancher so easily. He could feel it tugging at the rope which was still tight around his broad chest.

He pulled the pocket-knife from his pocket and unfolded its blade once again. Its honed edge sliced through the rope as easily as a branding-iron could burn through the hide of a maverick.

Adams felt the relief when the rope fell from around his bruised and bleeding chest. Within a heartbeat it was consumed by the water and vanished beneath the foaming river. The rancher steadied himself as his eyes burned through the moonlight up at the heavily armed outlaws.

Then he noticed some of them turning their guns away from Colonel García's direction and aiming them once again to where they had left Rip Calloway and the rest of their men earlier. A dread came over him.

Adams moved up through the rocks and squinted hard at the moonlit prairie. He could see Rip riding at the head of the half-dozen men towards the outlaws. Their guns were blazing.

'The fools!' Adams whispered to himself. 'What are Rip and the boys thinking about? They'll be slaughtered once they get into range of them carbines!'

Adams knew that he had to do something.

Something fast!

He tore at what was left of his shirt and let the two well-wrapped guns fall at his knees. As his gloved fingers untied the weapons from their leather bindings, he prayed that no water had got into the guns' workings.

This was no place to be with waterlogged Colts. They seemed dry enough but the only true test would be when he squeezed their triggers and the hammers fell on the bullets' brass castings.

Suddenly, as he was about to holster one of the golden guns he heard a startled voice call out above the deafening noise of gunfire.

'Look down by the rocks, boss! We got us a visitor!'

Before Gene Adams had time to turn he felt the heat of a bullet pass within inches of his face. He dropped on to his side and blasted both his guns at exactly the same moment. The scream of the outlaw echoed all around the rocks as his body fell down the steep incline.

'It's Adams! Kill him, boys!'

Adams moved like a mountain lion between the boulders as bullets rained down on him like a hailstorm. He recognized the voice. It was Lucifer's!

'Maybe you ought to try and kill me yourself, Lucifer!' Adams taunted.

The Bar 10 rancher could hear the sound of cowboy boots scrambling all over the rocks as the outlaws left the protection of their dugout and sought him with their lethal weapons.

'You're a dead man, Adams!' Lucifer's voice rang out above the sound of his excited followers.

'Not yet I ain't!' Adams jumped out and fired

both his guns over and over again at the shadowy targets that loomed down on him. He did not bother to watch the men fall as his deadly accurate bullets found their cold-blooded hearts. Like a phantom the silver-haired man moved through the rocks as his thumbs cocked the hammers of the golden Colts again.

'There he is!' A voice screamed.

Adams crouched and screwed up his eyes a fraction of a second before a volley of bullets tore at the rocks above him. He knew that there were still five of them left. Five ruthless killers who were hell-bent on destroying him.

Adams threw himself sideways between two large boulders and rolled over until he felt the ground beneath his heels. Only then did he straighten up and blast his guns again. He saw two men twist as his bullets tore through them.

'I'm still alive, Lucifer!' Adams mocked again. 'I figure you're running out of men!'

Lucifer blasted his Winchester all around the rocks as the rancher's voice echoed out.

'Show yourself, Adams!'

Gene Adams jumped out from behind a boulder beneath a tall tree and squared up to the venomous outlaw. His chin dropped until it touched his bandanna. His eyes burned up the distance between them as his hands cradled the pair of Colts.

'This close enough, Lucifer?'

'Too close!' Lucifer smiled defiantly.

A half-dozen shots cut through the air from the last of Lucifer's henchmen. Adams fell against the trunk of the tree as a burning pain ripped through the muscles above his knee. He managed to return fire twice before the men disappeared into the shadows.

Lucifer dropped down on to the riverbank and then waved a silent arm at his last two men. They followed him along the muddy trail to where they had left their mounts earlier.

'What we doin', boss?' one of the men asked.

'We're high-tailin' it outta here!' Lucifer replied as they caught a glimpse of the nervous horses through the brush. 'We gotta get us some more men if'n we want to get the better of Adams and García and the rest of them federal agents.'

The sound of thundering hoofs filled the air above the trio of fleeing outlaws as Rip and his riders drew in their reins and stopped the six dust-caked horses.

Lucifer and his men paused beside the brush a mere ten yards from the line of mounts.

'You said we would be rid of these varmints if we waited for them, boss!' one of the outlaws growled. 'Now we're looking at having our necks stretched!'

'I made you all rich, didn't I?' Lucifer cranked the handguard of his rifle again. 'All you gotta do is live long enough to spend it.'

'I ain't ridin' with you no more!' the other outlaw spat.

'Me neither! You're a damn jinx!'

24

Lucifer inhaled deeply and watched helplessly as the last of his once powerful gang run towards the line of horses.

He was about to follow when he heard the sound of a rope cutting through the darkness above them. Lucifer backed away when he saw the rope loop encircle the pair of outlaws and haul them off their feet.

'I got two of the critters, Gene!' Rip Calloway yelled out as he tightened the noose that had the outlaws on their backs.

Lucifer turned and went to move when he saw the blinding flash of the golden Colt. His rifle was torn from his hands.

'Adams! he gasped.

Gene Adams moved out of the shadows and smiled.

'At last we got you, Lucifer. At last the honest folks on both sides of the border can sleep peaceful in their beds at night without fearing that you and your scum will come visiting.'

'What you intending to do? Hang me high?' the outlaw snarled as he backed away from the bleeding rancher.

'That ain't my way, Lucifer.' Adams walked after the retreating outlaw. 'I'll take you back to face a judge and jury. I reckon they'll hang you nice and legal.'

For the first time in his entire life, Lucifer sensed fear as he kept walking away from the determined Adams.

'I ain't for hanging. Now or later.'

'I figured that.' Adams nodded as he slid both his guns into his still wet holsters. 'Reckon I'll have to finish this myself.'

The outlaw turned his back on Adams and looked straight at the distant horizon. It was an eerie sight. Lucifer knew that within seconds it would be sunrise. The sky was glowing as the sun drew ever closer to rising just beyond the point where the swift-flowing river disappeared.

Adams clenched both fists and strode across the distance between them.

'Turn around and face me!' he snarled. 'If you're thinking of jumping into that river, I wouldn't recommend it. Them rocks under that white water could skin a buffalo.'

Lucifer gritted his teeth. He allowed Adams to take hold of his arm and spin him around on his heels. His cold, deadly eyes fixed on to those of the rancher.

'You survived the dip you took, Adams.'

Adams released the outlaw's arm and rested his wrists on the gun grips of his pair of golden Colts.

'Only just, boy!'

Lucifer could feel the heat of the rising sun on his back as he saw the face of his sworn enemy light up before him. He said nothing as he watched Adams's blue eyes almost close as the light blinded him.

Then he acted.

Swifter than a rattler, he struck out with both

fists. His knuckles glanced across the rancher's jaw. First the right hand, and then the left.

With the sun casting long shadows behind his broad back, Adams staggered backwards a few paces as he tasted the blood in his mouth. Too late, he saw the boot coming up at him a split second before its pointed tip crashed into his ribs. An agonizing pain splintered through the big man. He steadied himself after the impact and spat blood at the ground.

Most men would already have been chewing on the dust at the outlaw's feet, but Gene Adams was no ordinary man. He was made of harder stuff than most.

Summoning every ounce of his remaining strength, the Bar 10 rancher threw himself at Lucifer. Like a stunned grizzly he bear-hugged the outlaw and knocked him off his feet. Both men crashed on to the rocks and then rolled down to the edge of the raging water.

Adams released his grip and felt his head knocked back by the powerful punch of the man beneath him. He clenched his gloved right hand and smashed his fist into the face. Blood splattered across the rocks around them.

This time it was Lucifer's blood.

Exchanging blow after blow the two men fought like wild animals. The advantage shifted between them equally as their fists sought and found one another's jaws. Then as Adams pushed himself away from his opponent long enough to stagger

27

back to his feet, he saw Lucifer draw his gun from its holster.

As blinding gunsmoke spewed from its barrel, sending its lethal lead ball within inches of the exhausted rancher's face, Adams raised his left boot and crushed Lucifer's gunhand under its heel. Then he felt the outlaw's legs wrap around his own and found himself falling as Lucifer twisted his entire body to the side.

'What is wrong, Señor Gene?' Colonel García shouted out from above them.

Adams hit the ground hard. It was as if every ounce of wind had been knocked out of his body. He could see the younger man scrambling for his gun on the wet ground beside them.

'Careful, Luis! This *hombre*'s still darn dangerous!'

'Damn right, Adams!' Lucifer scooped the gun up and fired at the Mexican officer. The bullet caught García high, knocking him off his feet. A plume of dust rose into the morning air. 'I just thought of something, Adams!'

Gene Adams rolled on to his hip as he watched the gun being turned and aimed at him.

'What?'

Lucifer chuckled. 'With García dead, all I've gotta do is take me a new gang down south of the border and take over his family horse ranch!'

'Reckon his pa will have something to say about that, boy!'

'Don Miguel is old like you!' Lucifer laughed even louder.

28

'He'll fight!' Adams warned. 'Fight until his last drop of blood!'

Lucifer's thumb pulled the hammer back until it locked fully into position.

'And if I kill you, the Bar 10 is also mine!'

The rancher's eyes narrowed as anger welled up inside him. His fingers moved closer to the grips of his guns.

'I reckon you were right earlier, Lucifer.'

'Yeah?'

'Yep.' Adams stared up at the barrel of his enemy. 'You said that I'd kill you, and I figure I'll have to do just that. It'd be a sin to allow an animal like you to live.'

'Now you're dead meat, Adams.' Lucifer stretched out his arm and gritted his teeth as his index finger twitched on the trigger.

Adams's right hand went for the gleaming holstered gun on his hip when he heard the deafening shot ring out. To his surprise, it was not the outlaw's weapon that had been fired.

Lucifer's whole body jolted backward in shock. His long thin legs buckled as his finger squeezed the trigger sending a shot into the ground at his feet. His glazed eyes aimed their confused venom up at the ridge and focused on the kneeling Luis García's smoking .45.

'But you was dead, García!' Lucifer gasped. Then he twisted and fell head first into the raging rapids. His body vanished instantly in the angry water.

Gene Adams crawled back to his feet and watched as his friend staggered down the muddy rockface and walked to his side.

'I owe you, Luis!'

The Mexican looked at the swirling white water, which appeared to get even more furious the further downriver he looked. He shuddered and then held his hand over the bullet hole in his shoulder.

'It is over, I think.'

Adams heard his men getting closer to them. He squinted down at the river.

'Maybe!'

'But surely no one could survive that.' García sighed.

'I did.' Adams rubbed the blood from the corners of his mouth.

The colonel shook his head and turned to face the tall rancher.

'He must be dead, Señor Gene.'

Adams placed a hand on his friend's shoulder and led him towards the stunned Rip, Happy and the rest of their men.

'Maybe I'm just old enough to want a body before I bury a varmint, Luis.'

Gene Adams had been right to be sceptical. An hour later a battered, blood-soaked body was washed ashore. It was Lucifer and he was still some-how alive. Torn to shreds by the rocks that lay beneath the raging white foam, the outlaw clawed himself away from the river. He rolled on to his back and felt the sun drying his bleeding body.

'I don't care how long it takes, I swear that I'll kill Adams and García. I'll make them pay for this. They'll pay!'

ONE

It had been three uneventful years since the infamous Lucifer had disappeared in the raging rapids far to the north of the Bar 10 ranch, and yet unlike the authorities on both sides of the border, Gene Lon Adams had still not fully accepted that the brutal outlaw was dead.

Of late, more and more memories of the bloody showdown had filled his thoughts and nightmares. Yet he had no idea why, after so much time, he should still be so troubled.

But the tall rancher knew to heed his own instincts. They had served him well over his three score years and never once betrayed him.

Gene Adams led his horse across the blanket of bluebonnet flowers and inhaled their unique fragrance. But even the tranquility of this remote part of the cattle ranch could not answer the questions which haunted him.

It had been too quiet on the Bar 10 for far too long. He knew that the fates had a way of balancing things out. For every good, there was usually a bad. Sixty years had taught him that simple fact.

You always paid.

For this was still a harsh land. A land that had a million ways to destroy you. It could destroy anyone who was not fully aware of their own mortality. Only fools thought themselves immortal in the West.

Adams was far from being a fool though.

No one lived as long as he had without being blessed with some unseen quality. Whether it was brains or luck or a mixture of both, Adams was still around.

Still a living legend.

The million-acre cattle ranch was the biggest in all of Texas and its prime longhorn steers were the most sought after by the Eastern buyers of beef on the hoof. For more than forty years it had been the jewel in the crown of the Lone Star state.

Gene Lon Adams had created the beautiful ranch and still ruled it with a gentle but firm hand. It had been carved out of a wild untamed land through the strength and faith of the still hand-some rancher.

Only one other had been there when it had all started. The wily, toothless and bearded man who bore the name of the Indian battle axe that he carried at all times. A weapon with which he was an expert. Tomahawk was the only living person who knew why Adams had stopped his quest westward when he had reached this place.

The reason was simple in its brutal reality.

For this had been where the love of Gene Adams's life had been massacred along with every other member of the wagon train she had been travelling with.

Adams and Tomahawk had heard the one-sided battle from miles away as they had been scouting a safe route through the untamed territory for the wagon train far behind them. The pioneers' cries of terror mixed with the war screams of the attacking Indians chilled both hardened men to the bone. Yet they had not been able to reach the settlers in time. By the time that they had managed to gallop back to where they had left the hundreds of men, women and children, it had been too late. The Indians had gone and all that remained was the remnants of what had once been living people.

That had been a different time. Another world.

The two cowboys had buried every one of the bodies they had discovered where they had found them. It had taken more than two days to lay them all to rest.

The unholy evidence of what had obviously been a one-sided fight was in total contrast with the strangely evocative hillside. Countless swaying bluebonnet flowers covered the entire area and even the blood could not mar their majestic beauty.

Of all the places Gene Adams had altered within the land he had called simply, the Bar 10, this was one he never allowed any alteration to. Countless

34

bodies lay in unmarked graves beneath the sea of flowers.

Adams looked around the peaceful scenery and studied the trees and snow-capped mountains far to the north. He had seen this place countless times over the years during the changing seasons. It still left him feeling in awe. For all his hard work on the rest of the Bar 10, he knew that nature had still managed to make something no mere man could equal.

This was the only part of the Bar 10 that he never allowed any of his cattle to graze. For this hillside of flowers was sacred. A place where he came to be at peace with himself and be close to his long-lost love.

Unlike most men, Gene Adams knew his own destiny.

Like all the rannies who had perished and been buried here over the previous four decades, Adams knew that one day, he too would be laid to rest in the most peaceful corner of his vast ranch.

It was the only certainty in an otherwise unpredictable existence. The veteran rancher stood silently amid the knee-high flowers, holding on to the reins of his tall chestnut mare as the sound of a galloping mount grew louder behind him.

Adams turned and watched as Rip Calloway drew back on his reins and dismounted in one fluid movement that only an expert cowboy could. Calloway pulled a letter from his shirt pocket and handed it to the rancher.

'Happy brung this from town, Gene,' an exhausted Rip panted. 'It ain't even gotta stamp, just some funny candle-wax on the back.'

Gene Adams eyes narrowed as he turned the letter over and stared at the ancient Mexican seal. A seal that he instantly knew belonged to the family of one of his oldest friends south of the border.

'This is the family seal of the García family, Rip,' he told the young cowboy as he carefully opened the envelope and removed the letter. He shook the paper until it unfolded and then studied the words. 'You remember Luis?'

'You mean Colonel García? The Mexican officer who came up here on a secret mission a few years back?'

'Yep, the same. I helped him hunt down a gang of American killers who had been raiding Mexican ranches. We got them all except their leader. He vanished into a real angry river with one of the colonel's bullets in him.'

'That letter from the colonel?' Rip asked.

'Nope,' Adams drawled. 'It's from his father, Don Miguel.'

Rip moved closer to the rancher. He had never seen the rancher look so worried before. Whatever the words said, the young cowboy knew it had to be serious.

'What's wrong, Gene?'

'Trouble, son. Big trouble.' Adams sighed heavily as he shook the paper. 'I knew that something was wrong. Something's been gnawing at my craw for days. This letter is the answer.'

'You ain't thinkin' of riding all the way to their ranch, are ya?'

'Darn right, Rip!' Adams nodded. 'A man never lets his friends down when they ask for help.'

'Don Miguel needs help?'

Adams face was etched with concern.

'Yep! He sure does. Ride back to the ranch house fast. Tell Johnny Puma and Tomahawk to get their horses ready for a long ride, Rip.'

Calloway nodded, grabbed the mane of his horse and threw himself up on to its saddle. He hauled his reins back, turned the mount and spurred hard.

Adams gritted his teeth, slid the letter back into the envelope and pushed it down into his pants pocket. He rested his left hand on the chestnut mare's saddle horn and then hopped up until his boot entered the stirrup and allowed him to throw his right leg over the hand-tooled saddle.

'C'mon, Amy. We got to go help a friend!'

The tall animal cantered through the swaying ocean of bluebonnet flowers until they reached the vast fertile grassland filled with countless long-horns.

There was an urgency in every stride of the horse as it slowly increased its pace in response to her master's encouragement.

TWO

The two Mexican cavalry officers urged their trusty horses ever onward through the dry, parched landscape. For days they had travelled from their military outpost to the lead rider's family home.

The famed García palomino ranch was an oasis in an otherwise arid region of Mexico.

There was an urgency in Luis García which his trusty companion, Pedro Cordova, could not comprehend. Yet, like all such military brothers, they never questioned one another when asked for help.

They were officers and gentlemen. Theirs was an unwritten code of honour. Something that was never spoken of but shared by every single one of their fellow cavalrymen.

García had received a letter from his father Don Miguel. A letter that dripped with desperation on every line.

Its words haunted him.

The two riders drove their mounts down the

steep slope and across the last of the sandy ground until they reached the lush expanse of grass. They continued on and on until they felt the cool river air on their faces. Soon the hot blistering rays of the sun were filtered by the leaves of countless tree canopies above them.

'How far now, my colonel?' Cordova asked, drawing his horse level with his travelling companion's.

'Another few miles and you shall cast your eyes upon the most beautiful ranch in all of Mexico, Pedro,' came the reply.

The two horses gathered pace as their masters urged them on towards their as yet unseen destination. With the scent of the river's water in the horses' nostrils, the two well trained chargers thundered on.

But all was not as idyllic as it appeared to the pair of weary horsemen. Their tired, dust-filled eyes did not see the threat that loomed on both sides. García and Cordova aimed their mounts into the well-used avenue of lofty trees. It was the main trail to the García ranch, which the colonel had used countless times in his life.

Yet its beauty deceived the riders.

The nine gunmen who had secreted themselves behind the trunks of the broad-leafed oaks had been waiting far too long for their prey to arrive to have a single ounce of remorse or even the slightest hint of charity left in their worthless souls.

They were ready to kill.

39

A rancid mixture of loyalty and fear flowed through their veins. They would obey their leader's deadly orders without a second thought.

As the two cavalry officers reached the half-way mark of the natural avenue, they knew nothing of the primed weapons which were aimed straight at them from both sides.

'Now!' came the voice from the shadows.

Each of the nine men squeezed their triggers at exactly the same moment.

The deafening volley echoed all around the normally tranquil land. No mere thunderstorm could have ever created a louder noise as the hammers of the guns and rifles hit the brass casings of the outlaws' bullets again and again.

Red-hot tapers of deadly lead burned the air as they homed in on the pair of stunned horsemen.

It was like the fourth of July, but these were no mere fireworks which ripped into the army tunics.

Acrid gunsmoke choked and blinded both bushwhackers and victims alike.

Relentless bullets tore through the shady avenue and ripped into the horsemen. Their horses reared up and kicked out at the speeding bullets. It was as if they were trying vainly to fend off the deadly lead shot that sought to destroy their masters.

Yet the accuracy of the vicious rifles had already done their worst. Now time was running out, just like the blood which poured from the cavalry officers' wounds.

The bushwhackers shots continued to seek and find their targets.

Colonel Luis García swayed in his saddle and felt another well-aimed bullet tear through his tunic and deflect off his ribs. He screamed out in agony but no one heard his pitiful cries above the sound of the continuous gunfire.

The outlaws' gunsmoke filled the air all around them as the superior officer dragged his reins up to his blood soaked chest and called out above the deafening noise.

'Follow me!'

'*Sí*, my colonel!' García replied as he somehow remained atop the mount which was drenched in his blood. His gloved fingers fought desperately to maintain a grip on the sticky gore-covered leathers.

Both cavalry officers were bleeding badly as they spurred their horses and drove them into the dense bush that fringed the line of trees. Somehow, even though their bodies were torn to ribbons, they managed to muster their unequalled equestrian skills and force their terrified mounts to respond.

The gunsmoke that had been spewed from the rifle barrels of their unseen enemies gave the wounded soldiers just enough camouflage for them to escape the crossfire and head off into the countryside.

The outlaws ran from the cover of the trees and stood firing after the fleeing horsemen. Against the odds, their prey had slipped out of their trap.

'Quit wastin' bullets!' Lucifer screamed out at his men.

The outlaws obeyed immediately and watched their leader stroll out of the shadows towards them. Although his face still bore the scars of his last meeting with García and Adams years earlier, Lucifer had lost none of his confidence.

He smiled.

'The turkey-shoot has turned into a coon-hunt, boys. Get the horses!'

THREE

If ever evil manifested itself in human form, it was in the abject excuses for men who spurred their mounts after their already stricken prey. The ten riders forged their way through the trees and brush after García and his fellow officer. None of the outlaws was a trained tracker, but they had no problem following the unmistakable trail of blood left in the wake of the fleeing cavalrymen.

Every few seconds the ten riders caught glimpses of the two Mexicans as they tried to maintain the distance between themselves and the ruthless bushwhackers who refused to stop their pursuit. Each time the outlaws spotted them through the trees and dense undergrowth they fired their guns.

Gunsmoke hung on the air until Lucifer and his gang drove their way through it. The chilling yelps of delight grew louder in the ears of García and Cordova as their murderous followers gained ground on them. Every passing moment brought the dealers of death closer and closer.

Lucifer was now at the head of his gunmen, with unbridled excitement coursing through his veins. He could not conceal the sheer pleasure that the chase gave him as the horse beneath his saddle leapt over every obstacle in their way. Like a wild animal, Lucifer had the scent of blood in his nostrils and it was an aroma that he recognized.

One he savoured above all others.

He spurred on and on.

The nine outlaws behind him somehow managed to keep pace as the trail twisted around the trees and began to head for the river. There was less cover here on the slope which led to the riverbanks and more opportunity for back-shooters to exploit their trade.

All the outlaws' horses crashed their way between the trees and leapt down on to the flatter ground.

Lucifer hauled back on his reins and shouted out as he pointed to the pair of half-dead riders a mere thirty yards ahead of them.

'There they are, boys. Shoot their damn horses out from under 'em.'

Before any of them could respond, Lucifer had hauled one of his six-shooters from its holster and fanned the hammer until all six bullets had been sent into the two horses.

He screamed out loud as the cavalrymen's horses crumpled beneath their masters, throwing the dishevelled officers to the ground heavily.

'I got them! Yee-ha!'

The ten riders thundered through the trees until they reached the fallen soldiers. None of them had ever witnessed so much blood covering men who were still somehow alive.

Like a pack of savage, half-crazed wolves the ten riders hastily dismounted and cocked their weapons.

Lucifer pushed his men aside and stared down at the two pitiful creatures clawing at the ground in vain attempts to get to their feet.

He was unable to disguise his joy at the sight before him.

Pedro Cordova dragged his sabre from its scabbard and aimed its razor-sharp blade up at Lucifer. It was a defiant yet futile gesture.

'Who are you, *señor*? Why have you done this?'

The outlaw leader roared with laughter.

'That's a pretty long toothpick you got there, boy!'

Lieutenant Cordova swung the blade. Its honed edge made the air buzz.

Lucifer holstered his empty gun, then drew the other. He kicked the sabre out of the blood-covered hand.

'Ain't bin a good day for you, has it?'

He cocked its hammer and fired. The shot went straight between Cordova's eyes. The back of the skull exploded. The cavalry officer crashed backward into the ground through the violent impact. Bits of his brain were everywhere.

Lucifer turned and stared down at the man he had managed to trick into riding into his well-laid trap. He hovered over the confused officer.

'Colonel García!' he muttered in a victorious tone. 'At last we meet again.'

'So it is the great Lucifer who has risen from out of the slime once again!' Luis García gasped as he managed to scramble back to his feet and stand upright.

'You thought that you and Adams had defeated me back in Texas, García!' Lucifer snarled as he carefully cocked the hammer of his gun until it fully locked again. 'I am living proof that it is you who is defeated, not me.'

García shook his head as he felt the last drops of his life's blood pumping from out of the numerous bullet wounds that covered his body.

'Is this what all this is about, Lucifer? Revenge?'

'Damn right! You and Gene Adams thought that you were the victors but you're both wrong. I'm the winner!'

'So this is why I was tricked into coming back here?' The colonel sighed. 'For you to tell me that I am the loser of a battle we fought so long ago? This is insanity.'

Lucifer grinned.

'I wanted you and Adams to know that you might have won the battle but I won the war.'

'Gene Adams will not be so easy to kill, Lucifer,' García warned. 'I would not like to try and take on that man.'

Lucifer raised the gun until it was aimed at the officer's heart.

'Beg me to spare your life, García! Beg!'

García smiled and shook his head.

'There is no point. Shoot and be done with it.'

'You serious?' Lucifer was taken aback by the sheer courage of the man before him. 'You daring me to kill you? That's loco!'

'My people say that we all have to die sometime, *señor*. What does it matter where or why? Or even when? Do your worst, Lucifer. I am beyond help anyway.'

Lucifer squeezed the trigger.

He did not miss.

The deafening reverberations of the shot echoed around them as García staggered and looked up into the outlaw's eyes for a brief moment. Then he fell forward and landed on to his face at the outlaw's feet.

'Now we have to get Gene Adams, boys!'

FOUR

This was a dangerous land. The scattered bleached bones of countless unfortunate creatures bore testament to those who had underestimated the deadliness that lurked unseen for hundreds of square miles, yet the riders of the Bar 10 rode determinedly on.

The trio of horsemen were headed for Don Miguel García's ranch south of the border in answer to the cry for help in his letter.

Nothing could deter them from this mission of mercy.

For almost two solid weeks Gene Adams, Tomahawk and Johnny Puma had seen nothing on the long sun baked trail except the occasional wolf and rattler. They had no idea of what lay in wait for them on a few miles ahead.

Gene Lon Adams rode ahead of his two companions atop his tall chestnut mare closely followed by the bearded Tomahawk. A man whose tracking skills were as legendary as he was himself.

Bringing up the rear astride his pinto pony, the eagle-eyed Johnny Puma remained ever alert. His hands were never far from the grips of his matched pair of Colts; he could never disguise the fact that he had not always been a cowboy.

It was said that it had been Adams who had given him the name of Johnny Puma, and a new life which the youngster was still grateful for. Whatever the truth, there was no more loyal cowboy on the Bar 10.

The riders hauled back on their reins and stopped their mounts as they reached the top of the high dune of sand. Dust drifted over them as they stared off into the strange landscape.

'Hear them shots, boys?' Adams asked, even though he already knew the answer.

Johnny Puma held on to his reins, stood in his stirrups and looked into the distance.

'We heard them OK, Gene.'

'You darn tootin'? A deaf man would have heard them, Gene.' Tomahawk rubbed his mouth along the back of his sleeve and squinted around the land which faced them.

'I figure it came from somewhere in them trees.' Adams pointed a black-gloved finger. 'What you figure?'

Johnny sat back down on his saddle.

'Ain't there a river over there?'

'Yep.' Adams nodded. 'And that's the boundary line for Don Miguel's spread.'

'Well I don't know about you boys but I reckon

we ought to go see if anyone needs our help,'
Tomahawk suggested.

'I think the old rooster is right, Johnny.' Adams
gathered up his reins and steered the chestnut to
the edge of the sand-dune. He tapped his spurs
and leaned back in his saddle. The mare
descended to the lower ground.

'You coming?'

Tomahawk's tongue rotated around his toothless mouth as he looked at Johnny Puma.

'C'mon, young 'un!'

The cowboys trailed the rancher down the sandy
slope and then spurred hard until all three mounts
were galloping towards the wall of trees that
fringed the wide river.

FIVE

The blazing sun glanced off something to the lead rider's right. Gene Adams hauled back on his reins, stood in his stirrups and felt a sudden chill trace the length of his spine as his eyes sought out and found the sight he neither expected or wanted.

He steadied his horse as his two pals drew up beside him.

Before they could ask why the rancher had stopped so unexpectedly, Adams said one word.

'Apache!'

Johnny Puma steadied his nervous pinto and saw the five braves use their bows to whip their painted ponies into action.

'Here they come!'

'Darn it,' Tomahawk grumbled. 'I hates them Apaches. They always shoot my horses out from under me.'

'Quit gabbing, old-timer,' Adams ordered as he gritted his teeth. 'C'mon!'

With the terrifying sound of the Apache war cries drifting on the hot shimmering air, the three Bar 10 horsemen dragged their mounts around and spurred.

With the haunting sounds of the Indian warriors in his ears, Gene Adams remained balanced in his stirrups staring at the distant tree-covered land that he had grown to know during his many visits to the García ranch as it got ever closer.

'Keep up, boys!' Adams called out over his shoulder to his friends as their mounts vainly tried to keep pace with the far taller chestnut mare.

Both Tomahawk and Johnny used the lengths of their reins to encourage their horses on, but with each pounding of their hearts, they knew the smaller Indian ponies were gaining.

Adams felt an arrow pass within feet of him. He dragged his mount to a standstill. With dust floating over his long-legged mare, he dropped to the ground and drew both his golden Colts from their holsters.

He knew his pals needed cover if they were ever going to reach their goal.

Cocking both hammers with his gloved thumbs, he carefully aimed beyond Tomahawk and Johnny at the approaching braves. He fired over the heads of the Apaches but none of the five screaming braves slowed their frantic pace. He licked his dry lips and then cocked both hammers again and aimed at their ponies' chests.

This time the Apache braves had no option

other than to stop.

Adams took no pleasure in killing any animal but had no choice if the arrows of the braves were not going to cut his friends off their mounts. The rancher made sure that each of his bullets found their mark. The ponies were dead before their painted bodies hit the ground, sending their stunned masters tumbling violently into the sand.

As Tomahawk and Johnny reached Adams he holstered one of his gleaming guns and kept watching the Indians.

'Keep going until you reach the trees, boys!' Adams ordered as he cautiously retreated to his own mount with his gun still aimed in the direction of their attackers.

Both cowboys obeyed the command without question.

Adams' eyes narrowed. He watched as two of the Apache braves staggered to their feet and lifted their bows off the hot sand before plucking arrows from their quivers.

He stepped into his stirrup and mounted. He continued to train his weapon on the Indians as they fired their arrows at him.

The arrows fell short and he released the hammer on his Colt before holstering it.

'C'mon, Amy,' Adams whispered to his horse as he turned her to face the dust left hanging in the hot air. 'I reckon them Indians ain't gonna give us any more trouble. They got themselves bigger problems. They have to find something to ride if they hope to get out of this damn land.'

The chestnut galloped on until it too reached the shade of the trees where his friends had stopped to await his arrival. He stopped his mount and then looked at the pair of sweat-soaked riders.

'I thought you'd kill them Indians, Gene,' Johnny said.

'Without horseflesh out there, they're as good as dead anyways, boy.' Adams sighed heavily, 'Besides, I ain't one to kill anyone just for the hell of it.'

Tomahawk leaned over his saddle horn and stared into the rancher's face. 'We was headed to where we figured them shots came from earlier, Gene. We ought to keep going before we lose the sun.'

Gene Adams turned and looked into the craggy bearded face of his oldest pal.

'I reckon whoever was doing all that shooting will be long gone by now anyway, old-timer.' Adams gathered his reins in his hands and ran his tongue over his cracked lips. 'Now I've unloaded my own lead, it's a certainty.'

'We gonna sit here all day, Gene?' Johnny asked, steadying his nervous pinto.

'Nope!' Adams said. He put spurs to his mount. 'C'mon! I reckon we ought to find a way through to the river if'n we cut a trail over yonder.'

They slapped leather.

The Bar 10 riders entered the wooded flat land at full gallop and rode for more than a quarter of a

54

mile between the trees before something caught the attention of the wily Tomahawk.

The oldest of the trio raised an arm to signal silently to his fellow Bar 10 horsemen. Adams and Johnny watched as Tomahawk reined in and dropped from his saddle to the ground.

Adams and Johnny hauled their own mounts to an abrupt halt and turned them to face the kneeling cowboy.

'Looks like the old-timer's spotted something, Gene,' Johnny observed knowingly.

'What you seen, Tomahawk?' Gene Adams asked as he walked his snorting mare back towards his friend.

Tomahawk glanced up.

'I got me some blood here, Gene.'

Adams dismounted and strode up to the man who was showing his gore-covered fingertips to the narrow-eyed rancher.

'That's blood OK.'

'Fresh blood,' Tomahawk added as he rose back up to his feet and rubbed it off on the seat of his pants. 'Found me some tracks too, boy.'

Adams stepped even closer to his pal.

'Where?'

The old man pointed at the grass at their feet and then aimed his index finger to their right.

'I figure that more than a dozen critters rode through here a while back. They headed towards the bend in the river.'

'Ain't that the direction where we heard the last

55

of them shots?' Johnny asked, taking a sip from his canteen.

Gene Adams toyed with the drawstring of his ten-gallon hat and stared off into the distance.

'A dozen riders, y'say, Tomahawk?'

Tomahawk lowered his arm and rested his hand on the hatchet in his belt.

'Yep. Reckon most of the varmints was chasing two or three other riders.'

'And them couple of riders must be darn badly shot up by the amount of blood around here,' Adams said knowingly.

Tomahawk scratched his beard.

'The trouble must have started over there someplace. Maybe a couple of miles from here. Ain't worth checking though, 'cos that's only where it started. It ended near the river.'

'That must have been the shots we heard earlier.' Adams sighed as he kept pulling at his gloves nervously. 'Do you think it might have been some kinda ambush, Tomahawk?'

The old man nodded.

'Yep. That would account for it.'

Adams looked upward as he mounted the chestnut mare once more. The sun was already far lower in the sky than any of them liked.

'It's way too late for us to get curious now, boys. We better head on for Don Miguel's. We might be there before sundown if'n we're lucky.'

Tomahawk climbed back on to his quarter horse and gathered up his reins.

'Good. I'm darn tuckered out. Plenty of time for us to go snoopin' in the morning.'

The three horsemen turned their mounts and cut a course through the trees which they knew was the shortest route to the river and the famed palomino ranch beyond.

A thousand blazing torches could not have made the Mexican sky more red as night started to claim what was left of the day. The sun was low on the horizon as the three exhausted Bar 10 horsemen approached Don Miguel García's whitewashed hacienda set in the centre of the lush grazing land.

The last crimson rays which traced their way across the large sky seemed to set the large, almost circular hacienda ablaze.

Gene Adams rode between his two friends along the wide dirt road set amid the verdant sea of grass. For the first time in nearly two long weeks, the rancher relaxed as his tired eyes focused on the impressive edifice.

'There it is, boys,' Adams announced with a broad smile on his face. 'We'll be sleeping on real beds tonight.'

'About time. I could sure do with resting my bones on something soft.' Tomahawk rubbed his bony rear.

The trio of horsemen continued to ride towards the strangely silent mansion unaware that every stride of their mounts was taking them closer and closer to danger. They should have been more alert, yet their weariness prevented their brains from recognizing anything except the sight before them. They had reached their destination.

Adams glanced up. As always, there were *vaqueros* on the highest parts of the roof tops standing guard as they had probably always done. He raised a gloved hand and signalled to the sentries. Neither responded to the rancher's gesture.

'I'm sure glad that we got here at last, boys.' Adams sighed as he looked to each of his pals in turn. They continued to steer their horses straight towards the building. 'I could sure use a hot bath and a hot meal right about now.'

'I'm a tad sleepy myself, boy,' Tomahawk agreed.

'A tall glass of wine might just take the sting out of my tailbone,' Johnny said as his young keen eyes focused through the fading light at the rooftops above them.

Tomahawk gave one of his toothless grins.

'Yep. Wine the colour of blood. I can almost taste it now, by jiminy.' Tomahawk's tongue traced around his whiskered lips like a pink windmill.

'I'd settle on a good cup of coffee,' Adams added.

Johnny Puma remained silent as he kept looking up at the *vaqueros* on the mansion's roof. The sunset was glistening along the barrels of their Winchesters. Yet the gleaming barrels were not aiming up at the heavens, but trained down on their unexpected visitors.

'What's wrong, Johnny?' Adams asked, concern

sounding in his voice.

Tomahawk squinted over at the pinto rider.

'What you lookin' at, you young pup? Gene's talking to you. Answer him, Johnny.'

Johnny was about to speak when a pair of shots suddenly erupted from the highest points of the mansion. The three riders watched in shock as the red-hot tapers of lethal lead cut through the twilight and tore towards them.

They felt the heat from the bullets and dragged rein. Each of the horses began to buck as their masters fought desperately to control them.

'What in tarnation was that?' Tomahawk yelped, trying to control his skittish mount. 'Was that the darndest pair of fireflies in Mexico or did some lowlife shoot at us?'

Gene Adams pulled his reins to his chest as the chestnut mare turned full circle.

'Who fired them shots?'

'The sentries, Gene,' Johnny answered and pointed up to the high rooftop.

Adams steadied his horse,

'That's loco. Don Miguel's men would never shoot blindly like that, Johnny.'

'I'm telling you that those two critters on the roof of the house shot at us, Gene,' Johnny shouted, focusing again on the two men wearing sombreros as they lifted their rifles again and cocked the mechanism.

Adams stood in his stirrups and stared hard.

'You're right, son! What's wrong with them boys?'

Suddenly the gleaming Winchester barrels spewed out two more lethal bullets. The hot traces cut through the air and sought their targets once more.

Without a second's hesitation, Johnny Puma leapt into action. Like the mountain cat after which he was named, Johnny had pulled his right boot from the stirrup and drawn it up until it was on the large leather saddle. He sprang across the distance between himself and his companions with both arms held out wide and knocked both Gene and Tomahawk off their saddles as the sentries' bullets rained down on them. Yet even though the young cowboy's selfless and heroic actions had taken less than the beat of his strong heart, it was still too slow in comparison to the venomous speed of the sentries' Winchester bullets.

Johnny felt the violent impact catch him high. Before he hit the ground he knew that one of the *vaqueros'* shots had caught him in his left shoulder. The sheer power was enough to knock the young cowboy off course. Johnny crashed across the saddle cantle of Tomahawk's quarter horse and went crashing on to the dry, dusty trail between it and Adams's terrified mare.

Johnny hit the ground hard and lay motionless as the mounts bucked in terror around his unmoving body.

Gene Adams rolled over until he found himself in a seated position beside the dazed Tomahawk.

'You OK, old-timer?' the rancher asked as he

caught his breath and drew himself up on to one knee.

'Gosh, that was sure sudden, Gene,' Tomahawk grumbled as he staggered up off the ground and dusted himself down. 'What happened?'

Adams's blue eyes darted up at the *vaqueros*, who were bathed in the last rays of the dying sun, and spotted the raised rifles. He reached out, grabbed his oldest friend and hauled him back down again as another two rifle shots ate up the distance beside them.

'Keep your head down, you old fool,' Adams advised. He drew one of his golden Colts and cocked its hammer with his gloved thumb. 'Don Miguel's guards are a little edgy for some reason.'

Tomahawk spat out a mouthful of dust.

'I already figured that out, boy! Reckon it was them shooting at us that give me the idea!'

'What's going on, old-timer?' Adams begged his pal for answers.

'Beats me. I thought they'd recognize us, Gene.'

'Maybe they would if it wasn't almost sunset,' Adams said. He watched the sentries carefully.

Tomahawk was about to speak when his screwed eyes spotted Johnny lying face down on the ground a few yards away from them.

'Look, Gene! Johnny! He ain't movin'.'

'Oh my dear Lord!' Adams exclaimed. Rising up, the rancher ignored the deadly danger that still lurked above on top of the whitewashed build-ing and rushed from cover to the motionless cowboy's side. Bullets ripped up the ground all around the rancher, but he ignored them.

'Johnny! Johnny! Speak to me, son!'

There was no reply from the cowboy as Adams turned the limp figure around. Then he spotted the blood in the last rays of the sun. Too much blood.

'Is he OK, Gene?' Tomahawk called out.

Gene Adams head turned. His eyes narrowed grimly.

'He's hurt bad, Tomahawk. The young fool caught lead when he knocked us out of the way of them bullets.'

'Will he be OK?'

'I ain't sure, old-timer.' Adams's voice was close to breaking as his gloved hands brushed the trail debris off his face. 'I think it's bad, though. He's pumping blood.'

Defiantly, Tomahawk ignored the risk of getting hit by one of the *vaqueros'* bullets and rushed to the side of the kneeling Adams.

'The dang fool! What can we do, Gene?'

Adams face was like stone.

'I ain't sure, old-timer. But we have to stop this bleeding darn fast otherwise he's a goner.'

Tomahawk placed a hand on the broad-shouldered man.

'You can do it, boy. Ya done it hundreds of times on the Bar 10 when we ain't been able to get a doctor.'

Adams gritted his teeth and inhaled deeply.

'I can't do nothing to help him out here when we're ducking bullets, Tomahawk.'

Then the two men's attention was drawn to the sound that came from behind them. They both squinted into the failing light towards the mansion and saw the half-dozen *vaqueros* riding out of the arched entrance. Even the half-light could not disguise the sight of the thoroughbred palomino horses as they galloped toward the Bar 10 men.

'I sure hope they don't start shootin' again before they gets a good look at us, Gene.' Tomahawk gulped.

'You and me both!' Adams drawled as he held on to his young unconscious friend. 'You and me both, Tomahawk.'

SIX

With the last scarlet rays of the sun behind them, the mounted *vaqueros* appeared to have ridden straight from the bowels of Hell itself as they bore down on the kneeling cowboys, their long rifles resting on their hips. The heavily armed sombrero-clad riders steered their magnificent thorough-bred palomino horses directly at the Bar 10 men.

Tomahawk went to haul his Indian hatchet from his belt when he felt Adams's gloved hand grip his wrist. The older man looked into the rancher's face.

'But they might kill us, Gene.'

'If we draw our weapons, I'd say that it's a certainty they will,' Adams drawled as his eyes moved back to the approaching *vaqueros*. 'Just stay still and pray that their sanity will return to them, Tomahawk.

'It ain't gonna be easy, boy,' the bearded cowboy gulped.

The horsemen only reined in when they saw the

familiar features of Gene Adams glaring up at them. Suddenly the palomino horses stopped in a perfect line.

A look of utter shock etched itself across the features of Don Miguel García as he stared down in horror at the scene his own sentries had created on the trail to his large home.

He threw his rifle to one of his outriders and dismounted swiftly for a man of his mature years. He crossed himself and then dropped down beside Adams.

'This is terrible. I am so sorry, my old friend,' he gasped resting the palm of his hand on the rancher's shoulder. 'Is Señor Johnny hurt bad?'

Adams scooped the young limp cowboy up in his strong arms and stood. There was a tortured expression on his handsome features as he replied:

'I ain't sure, Don Miguel. He's pumping blood like a stuck pig. We've gotta get him to the house fast.'

'We have no doctor here, Señor Gene,' García apologized.

'I don't need no doctor, Don Miguel.' Adams nodded. 'I'll tend him myself.'

'Let my men help carry him to the house. It will be much faster.' García snapped his fingers and half his *vaqueros* dismounted and rushed to the rancher's aid. Two of the loyal *vaqueros* took hold of Johnny between them from the arms of the Texan rancher and started back towards the house far faster than his tired legs could have managed.

It was a troubled Tomahawk who moved to his quarter horse and grabbed its reins before ambling to the chestnut mare and pinto pony.

'I'll take the horses, Gene,' he said.

Adams nodded silently and felt the hand of Don Miguel on his broad bruised shoulder again.

'I know it weren't your fault, Don Miguel. I'm just het up 'coz Johnny took a bullet that was probably meant for me. It hurts me to see any of my cowboys wounded.'

'Especially when it is Señor Johnny, I think.' García knew the affection the rancher had for the most loyal of all his cowboys. 'He is like a son to you.'

'Yep. You're right.' Adams nodded. 'He was wild when he first rode on to the Bar 10, but he's proved his salt more times than I can even recall. A man could not wish for a more worthy son.'

'Like my Luis,' García added. 'Fine men. Fine men.'

It was a physically weary Adams who tried to keep pace with the *vaqueros*. He kept smacking the gloved knuckles of his right fist into the palm of his left with each stride of his long legs.

'It should be me who got shot, darn it. I got me more flesh on me than Johnny.'

'I'm so sorry, *amigo*. But things have been very strange around here for many weeks now. My guards have had to repel many uninvited visitors since I received a letter from you.'

66

Adams paused and looked into the eyes of his friend.

'But I ain't sent you any letter, Don Miguel!'

'This is most strange,' García muttered as he thought about the rancher's statement. 'Tell me, Señor Gene. Why are you here exactly?'

'I got me a letter from you telling me that you were in trouble and asking me to come here to help,' Gene Adams answered as they started to walk again.

'But I did not send a letter to you either.'

'Somebody seems to be playing with us, my friend.' Adams's eyes darted around the vast dark land which surrounded the hacienda.

'The question is who?' Don Miguel smacked a clenched fist into the palm of his left hand.

'Who and why?' Adams added as they walked under the archway into the courtyard.

SEVEN

It had been only three days since Gene Adams, Tomahawk and Johnny Puma had left the Bar 10 and headed south toward Mexico leaving Rip Calloway and Happy Summers in charge of the vast cattle ranch when they had ridden into Harper's Fork for provisions. The two cowboys had managed to order all the supplies on Cookie's list before drifting into the Golden Slipper saloon for a few beers.

That had been where they had somehow managed to get themselves into their usual trouble as they met, drank and ultimately fought with cowboys from other cattle spreads. Even if Marshal Bill Cooper had not been looking for them, he would not have had any trouble locating them.

As the lawman stood outside the general store next to their fully loaded wagon, he could hear the fight directly opposite in the cowboys' favourite drinking-hole.

'Bar 10 boys in the saloon, Slim?' Cooper asked the store worker.

'Can't ya hear them, Coop?'

'Which ones?'

'Just Rip and Happy.'

The lawman nodded. He bit the tip off his long cigar, sat on the edge if the water trough and struck a match with his thumb nail.

'Reckon I'll wait. They won't be too long.'

No sooner had the words left his lips than the sound of breaking glass filled the street. A cowboy came crashing through the largest of the saloon's windows.

'Is that one of them, Slim?'

'Nope. That's Luke off the Cross T.'

Suddenly another cowboy came out of the saloon, sending its swing-doors flapping as Rip Calloway rushed out to finish the job with a right cross to the jaw. As Calloway dusted himself off and waited for Happy Summers to trail him out into the sunlight he spotted the lawman watching them.

'Look over yonder,' Rip said, checking his jaw as they walked toward the waiting marshal.

With his tobacco pouch hanging by its drawstring from the corner of his mouth, Happy glanced up briefly at the lawman and then headed towards the tailgate of their flatbed wagon. He ran his tongue along the gummed edge of his cigarette paper.

'Looks like old Bill wants a chat, Rip,' Happy

noted, pushing the cigarette in the corner of his mouth. He struck a match along his pants leg.

'I sure hope he don't want to fine us again,' Calloway sighed as they drew closer to the lawman.

'You done anything wrong?' Summers exhaled a long line of smoke and pushed the brim of his Stetson off his forehead.

Rip Calloway pulled down his hat to conceal his bruises.

'I ain't, but maybe it ain't me he's lookin' for, Happy.'

The seated lawman smiled broadly as both cowboys reached him and stepped up on the boardwalk.

'Howdy, boys.'

Both men touched the brims of their hats in reply.

'Can we do anything for you, Bill?' Rip asked curiously.

The marshal removed his hat to reveal the red, raw marks across his brow. His hair was soaked as he ran his sleeve across his temple.

'Is Gene on the ranch, Happy? I just gotta see him urgently.'

'Gene ain't been on the Bar 10 for two days,' Summers said through a cloud of smoke. 'He got a message from Don Miguel and headed south with Johnny and Tomahawk.'

'Three days ago,' Rip corrected.

The expression on the law officer's face suddenly showed his concern. He returned his hat to his head and rubbed his face nervously.

'He's headed to Mexico? I just have to give him some news that I've just had wired me from the authorities back East. It's a matter of life and death.'

'Whose life or death, Marshal?' Rip asked.

'Gene's!'

Suddenly both cowboys were hanging on each and every word.

'Say that again, Bill,' Happy said, dropping the cigarette butt on to the sandy ground 'Gene is in danger? Is that it?'

'Yeah, Happy.' Cooper sighed patting his vest pocket. 'I've gotta get him to read this wire.'

Rip leaned down to the lawman and looked him straight in the eye.

'What kinda trouble?'

Marshal Bill Cooper pulled the folded paper from his pocket and handed it to the cowboy.

'Read it yourself.'

'What's it say, Rip?'

'It's from the secret service,' Rip said as his eyes studied the long message. 'They reckon that some maniac is gunning for Adams and that Mexican soldier we rode with a few years back.'

Happy moved closer to his pal and looked over his shoulder at the note.

'I recall we both rode with Gene and Colonel García on some secret mission looking for that Lucifer varmint and his gang.'

'Yeah! We sure done for those critters and no

71

mistake.' Rip nodded.

'But why is Gene in danger?' Happy squinted at the paper in his friend's hands.

Marshal Cooper cleared his throat.

' 'Coz Lucifer ain't dead and he's got himself a new gang. He's hell-bent on killing Gene and the colonel, by all accounts.'

'Why?' Happy asked innocently.

'Revenge, son!' Cooper replied. 'There ain't no more vicious animal than revenge. It can twist even a sane-minded man and Lucifer was never sane to start with.'

'I don't get it.' Calloway shook his head. 'How'd them Easterners know this?'

Cooper chewed on his cigar nervously.

'It seems that this critter got himself jailed for something after he eluded Gene and Colonel García, boys. Got locked up for a couple of years. That's why nobody could find him. It seems he did a lot of talking to other prisoners when he was in jail. He busted loose a year back and has himself a new gang. They've accumulated a fortune in daring bank robberies planned by Lucifer. The other prisoners told the authorities of his plan to get even with Gene and the colonel.'

Rip looked hard at the marshal.

'Lucifer must be loco if'n he thinks he can come into the Bar 10 and hurt old Gene, Coop,' Happy joshed. 'There are nearly forty cowboys working there at the moment. Not one of them would let anyone get close enough to Gene to hurt him none.'

72

Rip turned and stared up at Happy.

'But Gene ain't on the Bar 10, Happy! Him, Tomahawk and Johnny went to help Colonel García's pa. Remember that fancy letter he had?'

Cooper shook his head and stood upright.

'It must be a trick, boys. Lucifer must be figuring on luring them both to the same place and then bushwhacking them. I've gotta try and catch up with them before they ride into a trap.'

'Reckon you'll need some deputies, Coop.' Happy raised both eyebrows. 'You'll find all you need on the Bar 10.'

'But can a US marshal do anything in Mexico?' Rip asked.

'This gives me official permission to hunt, arrest or even kill the critter who calls himself Lucifer, Happy,' the lawman said waving an official-looking document under both cowboys' noses. 'Besides, I like Gene, Johnny and old Tomahawk. I thought that I could warn him here, but if it takes a ride into Mexico, so be it. I'm game.'

'Has Lucifer got himself a reward, Coop?'

Cooper grinned.

'That's another darn good reason to head on into old Mexico, Rip. He's worth five thousand dollars.'

Rip and Happy looked at one another, then returned their attention to the marshal.

'Let's head on back to the Bar 10,' Happy suggested.

'There has to be a dozen of the boys around the

bunkhouse about now. I figure you'll get more than five riders to head on down to Mexico with ya,' Rip added.

'But you said Gene and the boys headed out a few days back.' Cooper was troubled that they might not be able to catch up with the Bar 10 riders. 'I'm worried we won't be able to catch up with them before Lucifer and his gang strike.'

'There's always the trail over Smoky Mountain and through Wild Horse Canyon, Coop,' Happy suggested, licking his cracked lips. 'It's dangerous but half the distance of the one Gene took. We might get lucky and catch up with him and the boys before they reach the big river.'

'What do you mean by dangerous, Happy?' Cooper asked, raising a bushy eyebrow.

Happy Summers cleared his throat and tried to describe the seldom-used trail.

'It gets kinda high and is a tad brittle.'

'Brittle?' the marshal repeated the unwelcome word.

'Yep. Brittle.'

'The trail winds its way around the side of Smoky Mountain and does get a little close to the edge sometimes. It has been known to be a little unstable,' Rip added, knowingly.

'Oh! That kinda dangerous.' The lawman gulped. 'Have many folks been hurt using that brittle, unstable trail?'

'A few!' Rip admitted.

'They weren't exactly hurt, Rip.' Happy

shrugged. 'They was killed. Don't you remember?'

'But if you say that it's a shorter route to Mexico,' Cooper inhaled deeply, 'then that's the way we go.'

'C'mon,' Rip drawled. 'There ain't a second to lose.'

EIGHT

Rip, Happy and a dozen of Gene Adams's other top cowboys had led the way out of the vast Bar 10 with Marshal Bill Cooper in a valiant attempt to try and catch up with the rancher before the outlaw Lucifer had a chance to strike. They had thundered across the verdant ranges like men possessed.

All thoughts of their own safety had evaporated in the hot Texas air as they spurred their horses on and on towards the most dangerous trail on the Bar 10.

The short cut would eventually lead them to the distant unmarked Mexican border. Yet this was not a route that men would normally have taken unless there was no alternative. For it was hard. Merciless. Deadly. It was rumoured that its red, sandy trail which twisted over the high unstable shale was tainted with the blood of its numerous victims.

Few doubted the dangers that loomed on the tree-covered slopes. Even fewer dared challenge it by attempting to use its seemingly ordinary trail. Smoky Mountain had claimed the lives of countless riders over the forty or more years that Gene Adams had reigned supreme on his cattle spread to the north.

It had become a forbidden place which Adams had deemed off-limits for all his valued cowboys.

Yet the fifteen riders knew that if they were to have even the remotest chance of catching up with Adams, Tomahawk and Johnny, they had to take their lives in their hands and risk heading up into the high pine-covered hills whatever the cost.

From a distance, Smoky Mountain looked no different from any other Texan mountain. But it was not the trees which made this high mountainside so notorious; it was the treacherous soil from which they grew that was so deadly.

If there was another mountain with such unstable soil, which could unexpectedly fall away from its high perilous trails and crash hundreds of feet down into the deep valley known as White Horse Canyon, the riders of the Bar 10 did not know of it.

Mile after mile the courageous riders had driven their horses on towards their distant goal until they were faced with a sight that chilled them to the bone.

Even the darkness of night could not disguise the awesome deadliness of this mountain.

'Are you boys sure that we can head off Gene by taking the trail over Smoky Mountain, Happy?'

Cooper had asked.

'Nope, I ain't sure, Coop. But it's the only chance we got at catching up with 'em.'

Each of the horsemen knew that Happy was right.

Only those with unlimited determination had even the slightest hope of survival on the trail that led over the treacherous mountain. They knew that even Gene Adams himself had a respect for Smoky Mountain.

With only courage to help them, they had continued onward.

They had somehow to cut three days off the long journey to Don Miguel García's horse-breeding ranch. Rip and Happy had said that it could be done, and yet as the riders guided their exhausted mounts up the trail they began to doubt their own optimism.

Could they really catch up with Gene, Tomahawk and Johnny in time? Was it possible? Could they even manage to survive Smoky Mountain?

The higher they ascended, the more they wondered if Smoky Mountain was not simply a natural geological feature, but a demon.

A demon which mocked mere human kind.

There was a storm brewing in the distant sky. An angry storm that spat out forked rods of deadly lightning into the deep Wild Horse Canyon far below. And it was heading towards them.

'This ain't good, Happy!' Rip Calloway said from his position at the head of the long line of riders.

'Reckon you're right, Rip!' agreed the rotund cowboy, who had earned his spurs the hard way, as he continued to steer his buckskin mount expertly over the soft ground behind Calloway. 'But it's too darn late to try and turn these nags around. We gotta keep goin'.'

'That's what's eatin' me. We ain't got no place to go except up,' Rip shouted out as he felt the cool air start to cut into his well-tanned face.

Relentlessly, the fifteen riders continued.

NINE

Time had continued to slip through the gloved fingers of the cowboys and lone law officer. There was more courage astride the fifteen horses that made their way up into the darkness of Smoky Mountain's trees than could have been discovered on most bloody battlefields. For unlike soldiers who somehow found themselves in other men's wars, these riders had all volunteered for this vital mission. Theirs was a glorious quest to try and save the three men who were the heart and soul of the Bar 10 cattle spread.

Even the weathered lawman had known that it was not the reward on Lucifer's head that drove him on with his fourteen escorts.

Gene Adams had more friends than he imagined and most would lay their lives down to help the rancher. Most owed him something.

The veteran lawman was no exception.

Marshal Cooper had watched the cowboys carefully string their saddle ropes around each of the fifteen saddle horns until they were all linked together.

They realized that if just one of their mounts lost its footing on the unstable trail and fell, there was a chance that the horses ahead and behind might be able to prevent a tragedy.

It was a theory that the entire line of riders had prayed would never be tested.

The higher the riders went up the treacherous trail, the more brooding black storm clouds gathered over their Stetsons.

The sound of thunder was growing louder yet none of the riders allowed himself to dwell upon the fact that the last place any rational person wanted to be during a lightning storm was on a mountainside amid trees.

Hour after hour they urged their mounts on until they had reached within a hundred yards of the summit. Few had ever managed to get this far. It had required a mixture of fearless courage, unrivalled skill and luck.

But their ordeal was far from over.

Smoky Mountain still had a few more deadly tricks to inflict upon the fifteen horsemen.

Suddenly, Rip realized that something was wrong. A cold chill that went through him was the first to alarm his senses and then he saw it.

It was like a phantom drifting over them.

A dense white fog came from between the trees

81

like a living creature seeking its prey. Rip felt his horse begin to shy nervously away from the cloud of ice-cold mist. It took every ounce of his horsemanship to keep the skittish animal under control.

'Easy, boy!' Rip soothed. 'Don't start getting yeller on me now. We've come too darn far. Easy! Easy!'

The horse snorted and fought with its master as the unearthly mist drifted and hung on the air until it was impossible for them to see the trail any longer.

Rip raised an arm to warn those in his wake, then eased back on his reins. He felt the horse steady itself beneath him as its hoofs tried to stop the ground from disappearing under the metal shoes.

'What's wrong, Rip?' Happy called out from behind the tall rider. 'How come ya stopped? Keep going. It ain't safe back here for none of us.'

Rip glanced to his right at the sheer drop. Even the light of the moon which had come out from behind the angry storm clouds could not find the floor of the deep valley into which he was looking down. 'I can't see the trail, Happy!' he shouted over his shoulder loudly as he continued to try and settle his frightened horse.

'How come?'

Before Rip could reply, the cold fog drifted over him and the riders who were lined up behind his mount.

Happy carefully eased his ample frame off his saddle and tried to find higher ground. It was almost impossible. He pulled at his reins and wrapped them around the trunk of the closest tree and secured them firmly.

'Get off your horses, boys,' he ordered. 'Nice and easy. Then tie your reins to the trees.'

One by one the men did as they were told. The fog seemed to be growing thicker as Happy scrambled to the side of Rip who was tying a knot in his reins after looping around the trunk of a thin fir tree.

'I don't like this, Rip,' Happy whispered, staring at the almost impenetrable mist.

'Me neither.' Rip rubbed his face and felt the icy chill of the fog biting into his features.

'I reckon I just figured out why this is called Smoky Mountain,' Happy said as he heard Marshal Cooper moving along the shale towards them. 'This fog sure looks like smoke.'

'You OK, boys?' the lawman asked when he eventually bumped into the cowboys his eyes could no longer see.

'Careful there, Coop,' Happy said. 'You almost knocked us off this darn hill.'

Cooper held on to a tree and felt the cold air freezing his lungs as he spoke.

'How can you tell, Happy? Can you see the edge? I sure can't.'

Rip licked his dry lips. He ventured a few feet up the slope and squinted hard. He had been afraid many times in his short but eventful life, and knew the bitter taste it left in his mouth.

He could taste it now.

'There ain't no way we can carry on until this fog lifts,' he said. 'To try would be kinda suicidal.'

Happy and Cooper grunted in agreement.

'What'll we do if we can't go forward, Rip?' the marshal asked.

Rip turned back and carefully made his way towards the lawman.

'We stay put, Coop. We have to just stay put and pray that it clears up soon.'

Cooper continued to hold on to the tree. He could feel himself shaking. He wondered how much of it was due to the sudden drop in temperature and how much was because of the terror that had overwhelmed him.

Finally he cleared his throat. 'I reckon you're right, Rip. There ain't no profit in falling off a damn mountain.'

Happy eased past the marshal.

'I'll go back and tell the rest of the boys that we're stuck here until we can see the trail again.'

Rip moved next to Cooper and then looked straight up.

'What you looking at, Rip?' Cooper asked.

'There's a moon up there someplace, but where?'

Lightning splintered across the heavens a few seconds before its deafening noise shook the fragile ground beneath them.

'Too close, boy.' Cooper gulped. 'That damn storm is too damn close.'

TEN

Smoky Mountain was well named. For throughout the year, whatever the season, the mysterious mist drifted out from the trees and hung like a white blanket over its summit. Few had managed to survive long enough to witness it twisting like a living being around the trees before enveloping the entire top of the mountain peak. Some said it was a natural thing caused by the high altitude and the trapped moisture within the unstable soil of the mountain itself.

A few had insisted that it had to be some ghostly apparition that no man with blood still flowing through his veins had the right to set eyes upon. For mere mortals had no right to set their unworthy eyes upon something which might have the mark of God or the Devil branded upon it. This to the insane or weak-minded was the reason so many had died trying to cross over the hazardous trail.

Only those who had survived knew the truth.

Some places are just plain ornery. Smoky

Mountain was the most ornery of them all.

Rip, Happy and the rest of the trapped riders from the Bar 10 knew only one thing for certain. They were at the mercy of the fog that had engulfed the high mountain tracks.

Trapped!

They were stuck on the side of the perilous peak.

The air had steadily chilled as time passed. Each heartbeat made the fifteen horsemen realize that Smoky Mountain also had yet another way to kill those who violated its forested peak. It could also freeze its victims to death given enough time.

The sound of distant thunderclaps grew increasingly louder and started to spook the already skittish horses and their masters alike.

Deafening noise rippled across the heavens above them and the bolts of lethal lightning came ever closer. The horses began to try and break free from their tethers as they sensed the approaching danger that was breathing down their necks.

'Keep them horses still, boys!' Rip yelled out as he clung to the head and neck of his mount. 'They'll drag us all to our deaths.'

Marshal Cooper had been the first to notice the break in the fog above their heads and the black clouds which were swirling around far faster than any he had ever set eyes upon before.

'I don't cotton to the look of that sky, boys!' he said as he too tried to calm his mount.

Happy had been sitting propped up against a

tree since the fog had set in over them. As it started to lift he turned and slid down the shale bank until he was beside his buckskin quarter horse.

'I reckon we ought to untie these ropes, Rip. I got me a feeling that we got us a better chance separated. What you reckon, Rip?'

Rip Calloway darted a glance at his pal. The fog was thinning as the storm above them became more ferocious.

'You're right, Happy! Let's get these ropes off the saddle horns, boys!'

The word swept along the line of cowboys faster than the blink of an eye and each of the expert riders removed the ropes that had tied the horses together on their ascent of Smoky Mountain.

As quickly as it had appeared, the fog was suddenly gone. The wind increased all around them and even the tall straight trees began to rock back and forth.

'This ain't good!' Cooper called out as he tried to stop his horse from breaking its reins and backing off toward the cliff edge.

Rip's hat was torn off his head and disappeared into the blackness below them.

'We gotta stop these horses from spooking!'

'But how?' Cooper shouted as he felt his muscles being tested to their limits by the terrified horse.

Suddenly Happy had an idea.

'We gotta blind the horses!' he screamed out above the noise of the howling wind. 'Blinker the critters! Horses are only really scared of things they can see. If they can't see, they'll settle down.'

'You reckon?' Rip shouted back.

'Nope! But have you got a better idea?'

'Nope, I ain't! But how exactly are we gonna blinker these horses?'

'Get your bandannas off and cover their eyes!' Happy ordered at the top of his lungs. 'Tie 'em around their bridles good and tight. Cover their eyes up!'

'What about the sound of all this thunder?' Marshal Cooper piped up. 'Won't the horses still get spooked by this?'

'Bar 10 horses have all been trained not to react even if some *hombre* fires a gun over their heads, Coop,' Happy answered.

'That includes my mount. Right?' the lawman checked.

'I reckon!' Happy said. 'Since you left your own horse back on the ranch.'

One by one the Bar 10 cowboys removed the bandannas from their necks and tied them over the eyes of their frightened horses. One after another, even though the storm was still raging around the mountain peak, the mounts calmed down and stopped fighting their exhausted masters.

'Now what, Happy?' Cooper called out as the entire sky erupted into a crescendo of noise that was so loud that the shale beneath their feet began to slide towards the sheer drop. 'We better do somethin' fast before we all end up down in White Horse Canyon.'

Happy knew the lawman was right. There was no time to lose. He looked at Rip and then back along the line of horses and their worried masters.

'Mount up! Fast as you like!' he yelled. For a moment there was a silence that was in total contrast to the lightning that forked from the black clouds a split second before the deafening thunderclaps.

'Are you serious, Happy?' Rip asked.

'You bet!' Happy nodded. 'We have to get over this damn mountain before anything else happens. We gotta ride before all hell breaks loose.'

Rip swallowed hard and looked at the trail ahead of him. He could see it every few seconds as the light of the moon managed to break through the angry storm clouds. He tried to memorize the way it twisted up towards the top of Smoky Mountain. He knew that once over the ridge, they were safe.

'OK! OK!' Rip reluctantly said. 'I guess we can't stay here for the rest of our lives.'

Happy turned and looked at the marshal and then into the faces of his fellow cowboys. Each face was etched with the mark of terror.

'Untie them reins and get mounted! Now!'

Slowly they loosened the knots in the reins, gripped their saddle horns and stepped into their stirrups. The shale continued to slide from under the horses hoofs as the Bar 10 cowboys mounted and lowered their weight down on the well-worn leather and gathered up their reins.

Rip Calloway eased himself on to his saddle and then tapped his spurs until the horse started to walk. As lightning flashed all around Smoky Mountain, the line of riders began to head up the slope in line.

The horses obeyed every command of their masters as they proceeded upward blindly. Faster and faster the animals ran over the unstable ground as their riders threw caution to the wind.

Suddenly the most violent of all the storm's explosions shook the mountain. A split second later a massive bolt of deadly white electricity forked down and hit the trees.

None of the riders had been ready for the massive explosion which tore trees out of the ground by their roots. A dozen sticks of dynamite could not have unleashed such fury or devastation.

Blazing trees and tons of burning debris rained down on to the stunned horsemen. They spurred hard as they felt the ground beneath their horses' hoofs give way.

Riding at the head of the brave troop, Rip Calloway had whipped the shoulders of his mount feverishly and galloped up what remained of the fragile trail. With every stride of his horse's long legs Rip could hear the screams echo out from behind him.

They were the chilling screams of both the men

and of their faithful mounts. Those who had not managed to escape from the curse that was Smoky Mountain.

'C'mon, boys!' Rip had yelled out. 'C'mon!'

If there had been any reply, the Bar 10 rider had not heard it above the continuing sound of mayhem behind him through the dust kicked up by his horse's hoofs.

Using every ounce of his strength and unequalled skill, Rip continued to force his horse on and on in a desperate bid to escape the storm's fury and reach the other side of what was left of the mountain before he too fell into the dark abyss.

Rip leaned forward and tore the bandanna from his horse's eyes. The cowboy spurred even harder and pulled back on his reins. He felt his horse leap up into the air, over the ridge and land on the other side of the mountain trail. Without letting up on his pace, he stood in his stirrups and looked over his shoulder waiting to see which of his friends had survived.

As his horse galloped downhill, Rip had seen only the dust from his mount's hoofs behind him.

Had any of his friends survived? The thought haunted the Bar 10 horseman.

ELEVEN

The nine outlaws watched the rider approaching their hideout near Alverez Falls. Fern Brunnel dropped from his saddle and moved towards the well-hidden lantern-lit adobe and the grim-faced Lucifer.

'I thought I told you to stay watching Don Miguel's hacienda, Fern!' Lucifer growled at the exhausted rider as he beat the trail dust from his clothes.

'But Adams and two of his cowhands showed up,' Brunnel said, a wry smile tracing his unshaven features. 'They got more than they planned.'

Lucifer closed the distance between himself and his top man and looked hard at the grinning face.

'What ya mean?'

'We done got them *vaqueros* of Don Miguel's so edgy that they opened up on Adams and his boys.'

It looked as if Lucifer had been kicked in the

93

guts by the pained expression that overwhelmed him.

'They started shooting at Adams?' the outlaw leader screamed.

'Damn right they did!' Brunnel nodded.

Lucifer grabbed the outlaw's shirt-collar and hauled him off his feet. He stared down into his terrified eyes.

'Tell me that they didn't kill Adams, Fern! I want you to tell me that he's still alive!'

'He is!' Brunnel's voice shook as he felt the fingers tighten around his throat. 'They hit one of Adams's cowhands.'

'Good!' Lucifer sighed.

'What's wrong? I thought we wanted Adams dead, boss!'

Lucifer hoisted Brunnel off the ground and threw him across the small adobe. The outlaw hit the wall and slid to his knees.

'I don't want no stinking Mexican *vaquero* killing that bastard, Fern! I want to kill him myself. Slow and mean. He has to know who has destroyed his life before I finish him off. He has to listen to me telling him how I'm going to take over his beloved Bar 10 ranch after I torture him to death.'

The other outlaws watched silently as Brunnel managed to force himself upright again and square up to their leader.

'But we killed the colonel darn fast. I thought he was as much responsible for hurtin' you as Adams was. How come you didn't make his death slow?'

Lucifer lowered his head and strode up to the outlaw with both his fists clenched in anger. There was fire in the eyes of the heavily scared man.

'García was just part of it. It was Adams who tracked me down and ruined everything for me and my old gang. Adams was the man who outwitted me. For that, he has to pay! García was just a dumb Mex who tagged along. I have to let Adams realize that even though he won a battle, it was me who won the war.'

Brunnel stepped forward and faced his boss.

'Some folks might say that this is loco. They might even say that *you* are a tad loco, boss.'

Lucifer dropped his right shoulder and watched the outlaw before him raise his left hand as if vainly trying to defend himself from a blow that never came. The swift left hook that followed caught Brunnel on his jaw.

The sound of cracking teeth filled the adobe as the stunned man staggered. Brunnel tried to throw his own punch but felt another brutal left hit him just below his ribs as a right uppercut lifted him off his feet.

As Fern Brunnel crashed into the wall again, Lucifer turned and faced the onlooking outlaws. He pointed a finger at them and screamed at the top of his voice.

'Let that be a lesson to you all! I can outfight and outdraw all of you. I'll kill anyone that crosses me. Anyone who even dares to question my motives. I want to be the one who kills Gene

Adams. He must know that it is me who is ending his life. That's the only way it can be. Should any of you kill Adams before I can get my hands on him, I'll kill you. Understand? The price of your loyalty is the García ranch and the Bar 10. After I have destroyed my enemies, they shall all be yours.'

'Don't you go frettin' none, boss,' an outlaw called Reno said for the rest of his fellow outlaws as they shied away from the furious Lucifer. 'You make all the rules and we obey them to the letter.'

Brunnel shook his head and spat out blood as he stared up at Lucifer from the place where he had landed after taking his boss's punch.

'I don't get it, boss. What's in this for you?'

Lucifer smiled and strode out of the adobe, into the darkness.

'Ain't it obvious, Fern? Vengeance is mine!'

TWELVE

The sound of the bullet landing on the metal plate beside the head of the unconscious Johnny Puma made every eye inside the hacienda kitchen return to the long wooden table with the large coal-oil lamp hanging above it. The white sheet that had been spread under the cowboy was soaked with blood. For more than an hour Gene Adams had worked feverishly with only crude kitchen knives in order to dig into the flesh of his young friend and locate the elusive lead bullet.

'More towels! More towels!' Adams snapped to Tomahawk at his side, as he tried to stem the blood-flow from Johnny Puma's shoulder. 'C'mon, old-timer. We gotta get this sewn up as fast as possible.'

'I'll check the poker, young 'un!' Tomahawk said, handing more clean towels to the rancher. The wily old man moved to the blazing stove and moved the cast-iron poker around in the red-hot coals. 'When will ya need this?'

Adams glanced up.

'Now!'

Tomahawk wrapped a towel around the handle of the poker and withdrew it from the stove's fire. He moved back to the table and carefully handed it to the rancher. Adams gripped the poker and lifted the towels from the still bleeding wounds. He then lowered the hot metal tip down into the wound. The stench of burning flesh filled the kitchen.

Tomahawk could not disguise his emotion and turned his wrinkled face away.

'Keep the faith, old-timer! Don't go all mushy on me now!'

'It just hurts me to see the boy like this, Gene.'

'You and me both.'

There were more than ten other souls within the large kitchen, including Don Miguel, his cooks and some of his *vaqueros*, yet neither of the Bar 10 men noticed. All they could see was the blood which had covered the end of the wooden table.

'Ya want some iodine, Gene?' Tomahawk asked, holding up the black bottle which had made his fingers turn bright orange.

Adams nodded. He grabbed the bottle and poured it into the deep hole that he had made trying to find the elusive lead ball.

'Get me something to sew up this wound!' he said.

Tomahawk's head turned and looked at the cook.

'You got any darning needles, ma'am?'

She nodded and started towards a drawer at the end of the long kitchen cabinet near the door which led to the rear of the magnificent mansion.

'And catgut!' Adams added.

Don Miguel García walked around the kitchen silently, watching the rancher at work. The Mexican began to realize why his son Luis had so much respect for the white-haired man. For Adams was unlike any other man he had met from above the long border with Texas.

Adams was cut from a different cloth.

It took another thirty minutes for the rancher to finish sewing up the wounded shoulder. As the large grandfather clock in the tiled hallway behind them began to chime, indicating that a new day was about to begin, García watched Adams stagger away from the table and sit down on a hard chair near the open window.

'Is Señor Johnny all right, *amigo*?' García heard himself ask nervously.

Adams nodded and then buried his face in his hands.

'Yep. Johnny's OK, Don Miguel. Now it's up to God. I've done all I can.'

García looked at the sturdiest two of his *vaqueros*, who had been hovering in the shadows for the entire duration of the operation.

'Take Señor Johnny to the closest guest room, *amigos*.'

Adams lifted his head from his hands and

watched the *vaqueros* gently lifting the young cowboy from the table and head off in the direction of the bedrooms.

'I honestly thought that I'd lost him there for a moment, old friend,' the rancher admitted.

'No doctor could have done a better job, Señor Gene.' García sighed. 'Where did you learn such skills?'

Adams exhaled loudly and leaned back in the chair. His eyes were focused on the blood that still dripped from the table top on to the tiled floor.

'A man learns many things when he's lived as long as I have, my friend. Leastways, he does if he's hoping to help a few folks along the way.'

'It is as my son has said many times, you are a great man.'

The rancher stood and looked into García's face.

'I reckon I've mended more busted legs and arms than most doctors. Dug a few bullets out of my cowhands too, but that was the worst one I've ever had to search for. It was right up to the bone.'

García shook his head.

'I am so ashamed. My sentries should never have fired on you without finding out who you were. I think that they felt my own fear and acted. It is inexcusable.'

The rancher pumped water into a bowl in the sink. Adams washed his hands and face before drying himself on the last of the clean towels. He then placed one hand on the shoulder of the troubled Mexican rancher.

'All we gotta do now is make sure Johnny recovers.'

The two men walked out of the kitchen and into the courtyard where the scent of countless roses disguised the smell of the stabled palomino horses. Adams rested a hip on a hitching pole and stared around the peaceful scene. He found it difficult to work out why García and his men could be nervous in such peaceful surroundings.

'Let's talk about the letters we both got, Don Miguel.'

García nodded and searched his pockets until he found the neatly folded sheet of paper. He handed it to Adams and watched him read its contents.

'This don't make no sense at all. I never wrote this, but it sure does look like my handwriting.'

García rubbed his neatly trimmed beard.

'Where is the letter that is meant to be from myself?'

Adams pulled it out of his shirt pocket and gave it to his friend. The stunned expression in García's eyes when he saw the wax seal made the rancher realize that they were dealing with someone who was extremely clever.

'This is my family seal, *amigo*!' García gasped. 'But how? I do not understand!'

Adams bit his lip.

'Both our letters are similar. Mine tells me that you are in trouble and can I come to help. Whilst your letter warns you that someone is coming to kill you. Whoever did this must know a lot about us and our friendship.'

'I do not understand how they could get hold of my family seal, Señor Gene.'

'Where do you keep it, Don Miguel?' Adams asked.

'It is in my study. Locked in my desk. I seldom use it.'

'Let's go take us a looksee, old friend.'

Both men strode across the courtyard towards the large windows giving access to the study. García pulled the doors towards him and led the way into the large room, with the Texan on his heels.

García struck a match and lit a lamp next to the ink blotter. He pulled out a silver key from his pocket and pushed it into the small, neat lock to the top left-hand drawer.

'Something is wrong,' García said turning his head and looking at Adams. 'The lock is loose.'

Gene Adams knelt down beside the desk and stared hard at the drawer. He then spotted a mark. He rubbed it with the palm of his left hand until scratches appeared.

'Someone has broken into this desk and then used wood stain or boot polish to cover the scratches, Don Miguel,' the rancher drawled as he returned to his full height.

García pulled the drawer open and stared into it. It was empty except for a scrap of paper.

'The seal is gone!'

Adams picked up the paper and turned it over. It was another letter. He swallowed hard as his eyes studied the words carefully.

'I reckon we found us the answer to our questions. This letter is addressed to me.'

'To you?'

Adams blue eyes flashed in the lamp light.

'Yeah, I've been played like a fish on the end of a line. I've just been hauled all the way from Texas with a hook in my lip and I didn't even notice.'

García looked hard at the tall Texan.

'What does the letter say?'

'It says that Colonel Luis is in trouble, Don Miguel.' Adams gulped. 'And if I don't do exactly as I'm told, he'll be killed.'

'Then we must go to his rescue!'

'Wait, old friend!' Adams muttered as his mind raced.

'There is no time to wait!'

Adams lowered the letter.

'This letter's from a critter known as Lucifer. The colonel and I had a tussle with this *hombre* a few years back. He's darn dangerous and a tad loco. But he's as smart as a fox in a hen-house.'

'I shall get my *vaqueros*!' García went to move away from the desk when he was stopped in his tracks by the firm grip of the rancher. 'What is wrong, Señor Gene?'

'There's one other thing about Lucifer I ain't told you, old friend.' Adams's voice was low as he continued to stare at the paper in his hand.

'Something darn important.'

'What, *amigo*?'

There was a long silence before the Texan looked back into García's eyes.

'The colonel and I already killed Lucifer once!'

'Then I think you should seriously consider killing him again!' Don Miguel said firmly.

Gene Adams nodded.

THIRTEEN

At last it all made sense. Adams knew that he and his friends had been toyed with by a supreme puppet-master. Lucifer had shown his hand with the note he knew the Bar 10 rancher would find soon after his arrival at the García ranch. He had already created the scene for his final showdown with Gene Adams.

A showdown that he had set out in the detailed letter.

But Gene Adams was angry. He had fought for hours to save the life of young Johnny and was in no mood to simply follow the instructions that the outlaw leader had carefully planned.

Adams knew that although Lucifer was a genius at working out bank robberies, stagecoach hold-ups and how to manipulate people, he had one major flaw in his nature. His self-regard would not allow him to consider that anyone would ever be brave or foolish enough to disobey him once he had set his plan rolling.

But Gene Adams was not a man to take orders from anyone, let alone a man whom he knew to be the most untrustworthy he had ever had the misfortune of tangling with. Adams knew that he and his friends had been played like fish on the end of an angler's rod.

That was about to end.

Now it would be Adams himself who made the rules, by breaking those made by Lucifer. The letter had told him that he had to set out at noon from García's mansion and then head to the isolated Alverez Falls on the edge of the horse hacienda.

It was obvious to Adams that Lucifer would have had no idea when he and his cowboys would actually reach Don Miguel's home after the long ride from Texas. The outlaw might have placed the note in the desk days or even weeks earlier. Therefore, Lucifer had to have worked out his ambush trap well in advance so that it would not matter when Adams eventually arrived at the falls.

Lucifer had calculated exactly how long it would take Adams to ride from the hacienda to the magnificent waterfalls. The rancher knew that it would be virtually impossible for the outlaws to lie in wait twenty-four hours a day. That was why Lucifer had insisted in his note that the rancher should start his long trek at noon.

That allowed him to put all his men in place at the same time each afternoon. If Adams followed his instructions he would arrive at the falls a couple of hours before sundown.

But the wily rancher had no intention of obeying orders for that very reason. Adams knew that he had to set out from the heart of the García ranch far earlier.

A few minutes before one in the morning, Adams had done just that and ridden out from the courtyard on to the fertile range, with Tomahawk and three of Don Miguel's top *vaqueros*.

The five horsemen were determined that they would reach Alverez Falls long before dawn and catch the outlaws on the wrong foot. To get the better of Lucifer, you had to try and out-think him. Adams had already had one brutal battle with the outlaw, of which he still bore the scars on his rugged frame. If anyone had a chance of beating Lucifer at his own game, it was the rancher who guided his chestnut mare after the three creamy-maned palomino mounts of the *vaqueros*.

But Adams also knew that however insane he thought Lucifer to be, the outlaw was still a genius who could create mayhem and then sit back and watch his followers reap the rewards. Those who rode with him were loyal simply because Lucifer made them all rich.

Whatever the letter had told him to do, Gene Adams was determined he would do the exact opposite.

There was no other way.

It was a slim chance, yet his only one.

Adams knew that back in the house Don Miguel

was clinging to the hope that he and his four outriders would be able to save the life of his son, the colonel. Yet deep in his heart, Gene Adams knew that his friend Luis was probably already dead.

Lucifer would have been unable to resist wreaking vengeance on the distinguished cavalry officer, if he too had been lured into the deadly spider's web.

As the five horses thundered on into the night, Adams wondered whether Lucifer would suspect that he would defy his instructions.

The outlaw leader expected people to jump when he tugged at the strings that he had woven around their very souls.

Adams refused to dance to anyone's tune.

The Bar 10 rancher would rely upon his own honed instincts to keep him and his fellow-riders alive long enough to find Lucifer and bring him to justice.

All he required was one more day. Maybe less.

The moon was big and bright above the five horsemen as they continued to gallop across the grassland towards their distant goal. Adams and Tomahawk allowed the trio of palomino horses to lead the way through the unfamiliar landscape.

'I thought Lucifer was dead already, Gene.' Tomahawk said as they followed the Mexicans down into a deep ravine.

'Everybody said he'd perished in the river rapids up north, old-timer,' Adams said as he teased his horse on after the creamy tails of the palominos. 'Make no mistake. He's alive and got himself a new gang.'

Tomahawk shrugged as his spurs kept the quarter horse up to pace.

'Say, tell me something. How come he don't like ya none?'

Adams glanced through the moonlight at his bearded pal.

'Maybe we upset him. Me and Luis did have a heck of a fight a few years back. We all got kinda shot up as I recall.'

Tomahawk nodded.

'And he got killed!'

'Luis thought so, but I never really could make up my mind.'

'Some folks can be darn tetchy, Gene.' Tomahawk frowned. 'I mean, would you like being killed?'

Adams urged his long-legged mare to follow the *vaqueros*' mounts as they sought out the shortest trail to the falls.

'Anyway, we got to try and nail the critter this time!'

Tomahawk raised his busy eyebrows.

'Yep. Not let him get away. Darn sloppy. I thought I teached you better than that.'

Adams nodded.

'Reckon you would have killed him. Right?'

'Darn tootin'. I'd have shown the critter the edge of my old Injun hatchet.' Tomahawk's bony hand touched the blade of his battle-axe. 'Yep, I'd have jumped in that darn river and trailed him until I was sure he'd drowned. Chopped him up like kindling.'

'You can't even swim, old-timer.' Adams sighed as he teased his reins. 'You get into trouble when you take a bath in a water trough.'

'A mere technicality, Gene.'

For more than a mile there was a chilling silence until Adams cleared his throat and looked at his oldest pal again.

'Seriously though, this could be darn dangerous, old-timer.'

'Yep. Don't worry me none,' the older rider said, and his beard jutted out defiantly against the cool night air.

'Lucifer is vicious. He kills like most folks blink,' Adams added.

'He'll try, boy. He'll sure try. Don't mean that he'll get the better of you and me. We've tussled with some tough *hombres* in our time.'

Adams leaned across the distance between their horses and tugged at the old man's beard. He winked.

'I knew that I could rely on you, Tomahawk! You've never let me down in all the years we've known each other.'

Tomahawk continued to look straight ahead.

'You figure Luis is dead, Gene?'

Adams was startled by the question.

'You starting to read minds?'

110

'You darn tootin', Gene. I seen that look on your face too many times. I knew when you was talking to Don Miguel that you didn't think we had a hope of rescuing his boy alive.'

'Maybe I'm wrong.'

'I sure hope so, son.'

The five horsemen steered their mounts a few miles along the ravine, and then the *vaqueros* cut their way up towards higher ground with the pair of Bar 10 riders in close pursuit. They rode for another few miles until the sound of the waterfall started to echo around them.

'Reckon we must be close to them falls, Gene,' Tomahawk remarked. 'Listen.'

'I hear it, old-timer,' Adams said. He screwed up his features and tried to catch an elusive aroma that hung faintly on the cool night air.

They continued heading south.

The trees thinned out again as they approached the prairie which announced the unmarked boundary to Don Miguel García's ranch.

Adams spurred his mount and caught up with the *vaqueros* and then stopped them. 'What is wrong, Señor Adams?' the top *vaquero*, Pancho Ruiz asked. 'We are not there yet. You said you wanted to go to the place called Alverez Falls. That is over there, a mile to the east.'

'I know what I said, Pancho,' Adams answered. He stood in his stirrups and sniffed at the air.

Tomahawk eased his quarter horse next to the far more impressive mounts of his four compan-

111

ions and scratched his bushy beard.

'You caught the scent of somethin', Gene?'

Adams lowered himself back on to his saddle. The light of the moon lit up his troubled features.

'Death has a smell like no other, old-timer.'

Tomahawk sniffed at the air and then looked up at the face of his best friend.

'Sure does, Gene. Reckon we found ourselves a body. Darn ripe as well. How far away do ya reckon it is?'

Adams rubbed his chin with his gloved hand and sighed as his eyes darted around the moonlit area until they saw the small outcrop of rocks.

'There!'

The five horses galloped furiously across the prairie towards the rocks. The closer they got, the stronger the sickly stench became.

FOURTEEN

Don Miguel García had not been able to rest since the departure of Gene Adams and his four companions. He paced around the large courtyard of his mansion staring into the concerned faces of his people. The lanterns gave the rose-scented area a warm glow which was in total conflict with the raw emotion that burned into the elegant man's very soul.

Until the discovery of the letter in his desk earlier the previous evening, García had not suspected that his son might be in mortal danger. Until that chilling moment, he had only known that his fortress-like mansion was being attacked by mysterious strangers for some unknown reason.

The attacks had always come at the dead of night. Shots had been fired at his sentries, as if warning him that he would soon suffer an attack that neither he or his sentries could withstand.

Don Miguel rested beside the ornate fountain that played in the centre of the courtyard and rested his face in the palms of his hands. He tried to fathom what was going on, yet there were no answers. For how could any sane man understand the workings of a sick mind such as Lucifer's? A mind that was ruled by only one emotion, the emotion of vengeance.

Don Miguel could not comprehend that all of this was solely because one man's vanity and self-regard could not rest until he had avenged his own humiliating defeat years earlier.

Suddenly a voice called out from above him.

'Don Miguel! We have riders coming.'

García stood and stared at the sentry. Another cold chill traced his spine.

'Riders?'

'*Sí, señor.*'

'Is it, Señor Gene?'

'No Don Miguel.' There was panic in the sentry's voice.

The elderly man moved as quickly as his bones could manage up the tiled steps which led all the way to the very top of the house. He stopped beside his nervous *vaquero* and rested a hand on top of the rifle barrel. He did not wish a repeat of the earlier mistake when young Johnny Puma had been cut down.

'Do not fire, *amigo.*'

'*Sí, señor.*' The sentry swallowed hard and clutched his rifle in his sweat-soaked hands.

'How many are there, Pedro?' Don Miguel asked, screwing up his eyes and trying to count the horsemen who were drawing closer and closer.

'Six or more, *señor.*' Pedro replied. 'I can not tell for certain for they are riding very close to each other.'

'Are they the same men who have been attacking us for the last couple of weeks?' Don Miguel leaned over the high whitewashed wall and tried to get a better view of their visitors.

The sentry shrugged.

'I cannot tell. I think they are gringos, though.'

'Our attackers have also been gringos, Pedro.'

'*Sí,* Don Miguel!'

García gripped the sentry's wrist and dragged his full attention to him.

'Go and get the rest of my *vaqueros,* Pedro. Tell them to bring the guns and be ready for an attack!'

The nervous sentry nodded and raced down towards the courtyard. His voice rang out as he aroused the rest of García's men.

'Who are they?' Don Miguel muttered under his breath. 'And what do they want?'

His questions would soon be answered.

Alverez Falls had been named after the first Spanish dignitary to have reached the remote Mexican waterway more than 200 years earlier. Since that time few men had given the magnificent waterfall a second thought. Yet this place had saved the lives of countless men and beasts since time itself had started. The ice-cold water which continued to flow over the waterfall never stopped crashing on to massive jagged boulders before running off into a deep lake at its base. Numerous smaller rivers started from this place and yet few knew that this was the source of the precious water they drank and which watered their crops and stock.

It had allowed life to flourish along its high-sided embankments and keep the arid desert at bay. Yet in all its long history, Alverez had never before been a place where evil was plotted.

Yet that was what had occurred as the twisted mind of the outlaw who only answered to the name of Lucifer finally began to see his plans reaching their zenith. He had already sealed the fate of Luis García exactly as he had calculated.

Unlike most of his men, Lucifer was unable to sleep as he continued to put the finishing touches to the fate he had devised for Gene Adams.

There were so many ways you could kill. So many choices that for once the outlaw leader seemed unable to make up his mind. He knew that he had to allow himself to gloat at Adams's misery. He had to torture the rancher far beyond any reasonable limits and still somehow ensure that his victim remained alive until the last precious drop of life fled his body.

Adams had to know who had finally defeated him.

Lucifer paced around the brush outside the adobe vainly trying to keep his mind focused. But the temptation to add one cruelty after another on the famed Bar 10 rancher was too great.

The moon was still large and yet he knew that the night still had at least four hours left before sunrise. He rested a shoulder against the adobe wall and stared all around him. It was a good hiding-place, he thought. Ideal for his purposes.

Set on the very edge of the prairie at the start of the thick brush which led to the top of Alverez's famed waterfall, the men knew they were within striking distance of Don Miguel García's ranch. A score of years of unchecked weed had almost engulfed the adobe, making it impossible to be seen from the flat lands which faced it.

As always, Lucifer had done his homework. He had managed to find the ideal spot to wait until he had started to weave his bloody plans together. From here, he knew that it was only a couple of hours' ride and they could strike out at the hacienda.

That would be the last part of his plan once Adams had been destroyed. Lucifer would lead his men against Don Miguel and then into Texas and the Bar 10.

The gang of ruthless outlaws with which Lucifer had surrounded himself knew that if anyone was capable of achieving the seemingly impossible, it was Lucifer.

'Don't you ever sleep, boss?' Reno asked the brooding outlaw who seemed to be muttering to himself as his eyes stared into the light of the moon.

'I don't need sleep!' Lucifer snapped as his concentration was disturbed.

Reno searched his pockets until he found a half-cigar and then poked it between his broken teeth.

'You must sure hate these folks bad, boss.'

Lucifer chuckled and glanced at the outlaw.

'Hate? I don't hate them none.'

'Then how come you risked ya neck getting into the ranch house to plant that letter in Don Miguel's desk?' Reno stuck a match and sucked the flame into the tobacco. 'I figured ya must hate them all if'n ya would take that kinda risk.'

'This is a matter of honour, boy,' Lucifer answered. 'I had mine crushed by the colonel and Adams. They destroyed my gang and thought I was dead too. Ya can't let folks do that without making them pay the price.'

Reno exhaled a line of smoke at the ground as his eyes focused on his boss.

'I'd have to hate someone to go through all this.'

Lucifer nodded.

'Most folks would, I guess. But this is simply me setting the record straight. You can't get away with killing Lucifer. He'll get you in the end.'

'Why not just bushwhack 'em? A swift kill and it's all over.'

Lucifer grinned again.

'Ain't no fun in a quick kill, Reno. The slower the better.'

Even ignorant outlaws who could barely read

the writing on their own wanted posters were smart enough to know that this was probably the biggest and most profitable job that they would ever take part in.

For the spoils were two ranches.

'Adams will be here tomorrow afternoon,' Lucifer said.

'Reckon so.' Reno could not hide the fear in his voice as he recalled the reputation of the Bar 10 rancher.

Lucifer rubbed the deep scar on his temple and then grabbed the cigar from Reno's mouth and inhaled its acrid smoke.

'You know something, Reno? I ain't slept one wink since I smashed my skull in a river after being plugged by García. My mind just never quits. I just keep thinkin' all the time.'

Reno swallowed hard.

'Reckon I must be lucky, boss. I ain't never had me no trouble thinkin'.'

Lucifer laughed again. This time it was a haunting laugh that chilled the night air. He continued to pace around the adobe again sucking on the cigar.

FIFTEEN

The stench was almost unbearable. A blind man could have found the two bodies that had been discarded behind the large rocks on the otherwise flat, barren prairie. Gene Adams brushed the flies away from his face then turned his back on their horrific discovery. He walked slowly back to his four companions standing next to their horses. The moon illuminated the pained expression that was carved into his rugged features.

Tomahawk moved away from the three *vaqueros* to the stunned rancher and watched as he lifted his canteen off the saddle horn and unscrewed the stopper.

'Bad?' the older man asked.

Adams took a long swallow of the water and then sighed heavily as his eyes trailed down on to the thin bearded man beside him.

'Real bad, Tomahawk,' Adams muttered. 'They been lying there for probably more than a day.'

'Any idea who the poor critters are?'

'Yep. I know who they are. We just found Luis and one of his army pals,' Adams replied. He returned his canteen back to the saddle horn.

The three *vaqueros* strode up to the tall Texan. They had heard his words.

'You say that this is our Colonel Luis, Señor Gene?' Pancho gasped in disbelief.

Adams rested his hands on top of his high saddle and nodded his head.

Tomahawk watched as the *vaqueros* rushed to the mutilated bodies and then turned back to the sickened rancher.

'Did that Lucifer varmint do this, boy?'

'Yep,' Adams managed to reply. 'He made sure that Luis died darn slow. I reckon both bodies must have at least a dozen bullet holes in them.'

Tomahawk spat at the ground.

'We gotta kill that animal, Gene. Kill him good. I reckon we had us ten riders around here, Gene.' Tomahawk walked around, staring at the dry sand. 'They rode in from the direction of the river. They must have dumped these poor critters here thinking that nobody would find them in a hurry. Then they rode off that way.'

'Ten of them, you say?' Adams growled. 'We wouldn't have found either of the bodies if it hadn't been for Pancho's shortcut to the falls.'

Adams looked up to where Tomahawk was pointing with his thin bony finger.

'Is that anywhere near the top of the falls, old-timer?'

121

'You bet.'

'There's a lot of brush around there, as I recall. You could hide ten men in there darn easy,' Adams opined. 'We gotta be careful we don't ride into no trap.'

Pancho walked to the tall Texan rancher.

'My *amigos* wish to take the bodies back to the hacienda, Señor Gene.' He sighed. 'But I will ride on with you to face these demons.'

Adams patted the *vaquero's* shoulder.

'Good man, Pancho.'

'All we gotta figure out is where them critters are hiding, Gene,' Tomahawk said. He ran his thumb along the edge of the Indian hatchet and stared across the flat prairie.

Pancho faced the two men.

'There is an old adobe that Don Miguel's *vaqueros* use when they have been rounding up some of Don Miguel's young horses.'

'Where?'

'I shall lead you right to it!' Pancho said eagerly.

'It'll be sun-up by the time we reach there, Gene.' Tomahawk pointed at the sky.

'Is there a trail that'll give us cover, Pancho?' Adams asked.

Pancho pointed to their left across the flat prairie. The dark line of trees could just be made out against the slowly lightening sky. Suddenly the *vaquero* went silent as he saw his two comrades carrying the body of the colonel towards one of their mounts.

122

'We better help, Tomahawk,' said Gene Adams. He removed his tent-gallon hat and hung it on his saddle horn.

'Do you think that the three of us can take on ten outlaws, Señor Gene?' Pancho asked as the three men walked toward the other body.

Before Adams could reply, Tomahawk answered the question.

'You forgets that two of us are Bar 10 men, Pancho!'

'And Texans, old-timer. You forgot that,' Adams added as he rolled up his sleeves and stared down at the body of the cavalry officer.

SIXTEEN

Fern Brunnel had only just taken up his position at the edge of the prairie on top of a large smooth boulder a few yards behind the adobe structure, when his sleep-filled eyes caught a fleeting glimpse of something tracing across the horizon. The rising sun was bright and danced across the dew-covered ground like uncut diamonds. The outlaw rubbed his eyes and blinked hard. It was enough to enable him to make out the three horses a split second before they disappeared into the dense brush a half-dozen miles south of his high vantage point.

With lightning speed, Brunnel cracked the hand guard of his Winchester and sent a bullet splintering in the riders' direction.

He knew that his bullet would fall short but it would also warn the trio of horsemen that they had been spotted.

'What you firing at, Fern?' Lucifer's voice called out as the outlaw leader strode towards him clutching his own rifle across his chest.

'Riders, boss.' Brunnel replied, pointing the long barrel of his smoking rifle to where he had seen the riders. 'I just caught me a glimpse of three varmints as they rode into the brush.'

Lucifer gritted his teeth.

'How far away?'

'Five miles or so,' Brunnel guessed.

Lucifer waved his arm and watched as Brunnel slid down the boulder until he was standing next to him.

'Can you describe any of them?'

Brunnel ran a thumbnail along his whiskered jawline.

'They was too far away, boss. But the lead horse was a palomino.'

Lucifer snorted thoughtfully.

'Were they all palominos?'

'Nope. Just the lead horse. Had a tail the colour of milk.'

There was a long silence as the outlaw leader brooded over the information he had been given. He hated to admit it, but knew that Adams had defied the detailed instructions in the note he had left in the hacienda.

'The rider of the palomino must be one of Don Miguel's *vaqueros*, Fern,' he opined. 'The other two have to be Gene Adams and one of his Bar 10 cowboys.'

'But I thought you said Adams wouldn't be getting here until just before sundown, boss?'

Lucifer nodded angrily.

'Adams never was one to follow orders! Reckon he figured he could get the drop on us.'

'Then what'll we do?' Brunnel asked anxiously.

'Get the boys out of their bedrolls, Fern. I figure that we got us some guests coming. We ought to prepare a reception committee for them and rustle up some breakfast.'

Fern Brunnel grinned.

'Yeah! What ya figure them bastards eat?'

Lucifer led the outlaw back towards the adobe and cranked the mechanism of his Winchester.

'The same as everyone else. They'll eat our lead, Fern!'

The three lathered-up horses cut their way through the untamed brush and between the tall trees as rays of the morning sun filtered down from the high canopy above them. Adams stood in his stirrups to take the weight off his mount's shoulders as he drew level with the *vaquero* who had led the way since they had left the small outcrop of rocks out on the prairie.

The rancher leaned across and patted the rider's shoulder.

'Pancho! I thought I saw something!' Adams called out.

All three mounts stopped.

'What is wrong?' the *vaquero* asked, steadying the palomino.

'Like I said, I reckon I saw something!' Adams

replied as he dismounted. 'Stay here, Pancho.'

Tomahawk wrapped his reins around his saddle horn and dropped down from his quarter horse.

'What ya seen, Gene?'

'Hush up, old-timer,' Gene Adams answered. He pushed one of his gloved hands into the beard and with the other drew one of his golden Colts from its holster. 'Ya want to get us shot?'

'Ya seen one of them bushwhackin' varmints?' Tomahawk whispered as he pulled his hatchet from his belt.

Adams moved his head and gestured for the older cowboy to follow. Both men crouched down and made their way through the tall grass. They manoeuvred themselves between the thick brush and trees until the rancher paused.

'There he is, old-timer,' Adams whispered. 'Near the tree.'

'I see him,' said Tomahawk as he too spotted the solitary outlaw sitting against a tree-trunk with his Winchester across his lap. Suddenly, as the outlaw moved, a shaft of sunlight glanced off the long barrel of the rifle.

'Is that what ya seen, Gene?' Tomahawk asked. 'That beam of sunlight?'

'Yep!' Adams nodded. 'Lucky for us that outlaw must keep that rifle of his well polished.'

Gene Adams leaned down until his mouth was against his pal's ear.

'Lucifer must have sent that critter out here to keep guard.'

'But is the critter alone?'

'Good question! I sure wish I knew the answer!' Adams aimed his gun at the outlaw and cocked its hammer.

'Ya gonna shoot the varmint?'

'You bet.' Adams bit his dry lower lip.

'You can't use your gun, Gene!' Tomahawk said, pushing Adams's weapon down. 'I know one of them outlaws took a shot at us when we rode in here, but they ain't exactly sure where we are, are they? Fire that hogleg and they'll swarm over us.'

'Then what do you suggest, old-timer,' asked Adams. 'He's too far away for us to creep up on him.'

'This'll do the job, sonny.' Tomahawk raised his hatchet and ran his thumb along its deadly edge. 'Nice and quiet!'

Adams watched Tomahawk as he leaned back and then hurled the axe with all his strength at the outlaw.

The tomahawk flew through the air at ferocious speed and with lethal accuracy.

Gene Adams watched in awe as the hatchet buried itself deep in the outlaw's chest. The body slid lifelessly on to its side.

'I got me a feeling that he ain't ever gonna finish that dream, Tomahawk.'

'Ya darn tootin', boy!'

SEVENTEEN

The two Bar 10 veterans led the *vaquero* slowly away from the outlaw's body, through the dense under-growth until they reached the bank of the wide fast-flowing river. Adams reined in and stared from atop his tall chestnut mare into the bright sunlight. He signalled to his companions as they brought their mounts slowly to a halt beside him. Tomahawk and Pancho squinted until they too focused on the foaming water a mile or so ahead of them. They knew that that had to be the very top of the high Alverez Falls.

'You still figure this is the best way to get the drop on them outlaws, Gene?' Tomahawk asked as he steered the black quarter horse next to the mare.

Adams gritted his teeth.

'I ain't sure, old-timer. All I know for sure is that they know we're coming.'

'But there are only nine of them left now,' said

Tomahawk his eyes wrinkling up proudly.

'Still too many, *amigos*,' said Pancho.

'I'm starting to think that you might be right, Pancho,' Adams agreed with a wry raising of an eyebrow.

Suddenly the rancher heard something in the undergrowth. He swung his mount full circle as his companions raised themselves off their saddles and balanced in their stirrups.

'Hear that?'

The unmistakable sound of branches breaking underfoot filled the ears of the *vaquero* and Tomahawk.

'Three of them, Gene.'

Adams knew better than to question the older man.

'Where?'

Tomahawk eased his horse next to the mare and then pointed in the direction of the waterfall.

'Thataway!'

'How far away are they, old-timer?'

There was no time to answer the question. Rifle bullets cut through the undergrowth at the three horsemen.

As hot lead passed within inches of him, Adams spurred and drove the horse back up the riverbank and into the cover of the woodland. As his gloved hands gripped the reins firmly, he looked back over his shoulder at his two companions as they thundered in his wake.

Then the trunk of a tree to his right exploded as

130

Winchester bullets tore into the bark. The rancher felt the hot splinters fill his eyes as the mare stumbled beneath him.

Adams felt himself continue to move forward as his mount came to an abrupt halt. He hit the ground hard and rolled through bushes until a rock abruptly stopped him.

The shots continued to deafen him as he tried to rid his eyes of the burning slivers of wood.

'Stay down, Gene!' Tomahawk's voice yelled out as he heard the two mounts gallop up to him before their masters quickly dismounted beside him.

'I can't see, Tomahawk!' Adams growled as he kept rubbing his eyes with his gloved fingers.

'Here, Señor Gene!' Pancho said, pushing the familiar shape of a canteen into his hands. 'Wash your eyes with this whilst me and the ancient one try to keep the bandits from getting any closer.'

Never in his worst nightmares had Adams imagined how painful mere splinters could be. He clumsily unscrewed the canteen stopper, lifting the vessel and poured water into his streaming eyes. The cold water felt good as he forced himself to blink until the pain eventually eased.

'Are you better, *amigo*?' the *vaquero* asked as he continued to cock and fire his Colt in the outlaws' direction.

Adams rested the canteen on the ground and nodded.

'Leastways I can see again.'

'You gonna start shootin' soon, boy?' Tomahawk yelled out above the sound of the rifle bullets as he fired his gun over and over.

'Reckon so!' Adams replied. He pulled one of his golden Colts from its holster and cocked its hammer back. 'We'll be here all day if we have to wait for you to hit anything with that rusty old gun of yours.'

Ferocious venom blasted from the barrel of the golden gun as the rancher displayed his deadly accuracy in keeping the heads of the three outlaws down.

'Two more riders heading in from the left, Gene,' Tomahawk gulped as he clutched his axe in his thin bony hand.

'I see them!' Adams said. He drew his other gun and cocked its hammer fully.

The pair of mounted outlaws opened up with their weaponry as they closed the distance between them.

'We got us a damn fight on our hands, old-timer,' Adams said. He continued to squeeze his triggers and haul back on his gun hammers.

The three outlaws directly in front of them started blasting again. This time their shots were more accurate. Pancho staggered back and then fell at the rancher's feet.

'Pancho!' Adams exclaimed.

The *vaquero* looked up and tried to smile as blood appeared on his shirt front.

'I think it is not very bad, *amigo*.'

Adams tossed his guns into Tomahawk's hands.

'Load my guns, old-timer.'

Tomahawk nodded and watched Adams kneel down beside their wounded friend. He then started to reload the golden guns with bullets from his own belt.

Adams leaned over the *vaquero* and pulled the blood-soaked shirt away from the heaving chest. The bullet hole was small and neat and pumping blood. The rancher lifted Pancho's hand and pressed it on the wound.

'Keep that there, son. It'll slow the flow of blood.'

'Is it bad, Señor Gene?'

Adams patted the man's face.

'You'll live, Pancho,' he lied as Tomahawk handed him the loaded golden guns once again. 'Just lie still and everything will be OK.'

Pancho's eyes suddenly glazed over. His entire body seemed to shake for a split second before his head rolled sideways.

'How is he, Gene?' Tomahawk asked as he ducked under the bullets that tore through the air towards them.

Gene Adams moved next to his friend and cocked both hammers. He let out a slow sigh.

'Pancho's dead, old-timer!'

Tomahawk gasped and looked down behind them. He was about to speak when Adams rose to his feet and started shooting one gun after the other at the five outlaws in turn.

133

Within a mere few seconds, Adams's lethal accuracy had taken riders off their mounts. His eyes narrowed as he watched the lifeless bodies crash into the undergrowth as their horses bucked in terror.

Yet Adams felt no satisfaction as he turned his attention back to the other outlaws who were continuing to fire at him and Tomahawk.

The rancher then stepped over a tree-root and aimed both barrels at the three men concealed ahead of him.

With each shot, Adams took a step closer to the men who were trying to kill him and his pal. Men who had already slain the quiet *vaquero*.

'You gone loco, boy?' Tomahawk screamed before loading his own gun and moving after the defiant rancher.

'Not loco, Tomahawk!' Adams retorted. 'Just angry!'

The outlaws now had to face their enemies head on as Adams moved closer and closer. His bullets had destroyed most of the cover behind which they had been hiding.

One by one they rose up and fired into the gunsmoke-choked distance which separated the Bar 10 men from themselves.

Shot after shot from the golden Colts bore down on the outlaws who had been sent by Lucifer to capture Adams and kill anyone who was with him.

Yet they no longer heeded the orders given to them back at the adobe by Lucifer. They knew that there was only one way to stop the tall Texan.

They had to kill him!

But Gene Adams had been an expert with his famed guns long before any of them had ever been born. For every bullet that left their weapons, Adams returned one from his smoking gun barrels.

A bullet tore the large hat from Adams's head but he kept on walking and firing. Then he stopped and lowered his guns to his side.

Tomahawk came through the tall grass with his gun in his hands and stood beside the rancher. He blinked hard as the gunsmoke gradually cleared.

'Where'd them varmints go, Gene?'

Gene Adams plucked his Stetson off the ground, turned and looked around the clearing until he spotted their horses.

'Did they high-tail it, boy?' Tomahawk asked again.

'Get the horses,' said Adams. He shook the spent shells from the hot chambers of his guns.

'Didn't ya hear me? Where'd them critters go, Gene?'

'They're dead, Tomahawk!' Adams drawled. 'Now go and get our horses!'

Tomahawk sighed and started for their horses. He tilted his head and looked back at the troubled rancher.

'Four of them left, huh?'

'Yep!' Adams nodded. 'Now all we gotta do is find them four other outlaws and try to kill them before they kill us, old timer.'

Tomahawk paused beside the tall chestnut mare and gathered up its reins. His wrinkled eyes watched Adams stride towards him.

'Was any of them varmints this Lucifer critter, Gene?'

Adams accepted the reins from his pal.

'Nope. He ain't the sort to risk his own neck when he's got hired guns to do his dirty work for him.'

Tomahawk mounted his black quarter horse and screwed up his eyes as he studied the ground.

'I could backtrack them outlaws' trail until we get to their hideout, boy.'

Gene Adams stepped into his stirrup and hoisted himself on to the saddle.

'I ain't doubting your tracking skills, but Lucifer would expect that. We gotta come up with something he wouldn't expect, Tomahawk. We have to out-think him.'

Tomahawk leaned over and rested a hand on the rancher's shoulder.

'Then we ought to head out of here and back to the prairie, boy. Ride a loop on the critters. Just like we do when our longhorns stampede.'

Adams looked at his weathered friend.

'Reckon that'd work?'

'Yep. I sure do.' Tomahawk smiled.

Adams tugged at the jutting beard and grinned.

'It's worth a try. C'mon, partner. We got us some varmints to round up!'

Tomahawk reached out, grabbed the rancher's sleeve and winked.

'Ya knows what'd really confuse the outlaws, boy?'

Adams steadied his horse.

'Nope. What'd confuse 'em?'

The older rider reached back to his saddlebags and poked a thin hand into one of the satchels. He pulled out a half-full sack of flour and showed it to Adams.

'Got some paper, Gene?'

Adams raised an eyebrow as he too reached back into one of the satchels of his saddlebags. He pulled out two sheets of crumpled paper.

'Just these old feed bills.'

'That'll do.' Tomahawk took the paper and then plucked the last of his bullets from his gunbelt. 'What ya reckon Lucifer will think when he hears these bullets explode?'

Gene Adams smiled and watched Tomahawk drop the bullets into the flour sack and then push the paper on top.

'Would you like a match?'

'Ya darn tootin'!' Tomahawk accepted the match, dragged its tip across his saddle horn, then set light to the paper in the sack. The older horseman then carefully lowered the sack on to the ground. 'We ought to be a mile or so away from here when that flour fires up enough heat to pop them bullets.'

'You ain't as dumb as you look!' Adams laughed.

'Lucifer is gonna think we're still here!'

'C'mon, Gene! We gotta get out of here!' Tomahawk nodded.

Both riders used their reins to slap the shoulders of their mounts. Within a heartbeat they had left the burning sack far behind them knowing that when its contents did finally explode into action, they should be far away. The horses thundered through the trees towards the prairie once more.

After battling their way valiantly through the razor sharp brush that lined the riverbank on its way towards the sheer drop of the waterfall, Tomahawk and Adams had only just cleared the trees and were turning their horses on the dry arid sand of the prairie when a volley of rifle fire blasted in their direction from the head of the falls. One bullet ripped through the reins of the black quarter horse as the other came close enough to Adams's face that it burned his tanned skin.

Both stunned riders toppled from their saddles and hit the ground hard.

'What in tarnation?' gasped Tomahawk as he rubbed the sand from his beard and tried to see where the shots had come from.

Gene Adams pushed himself up and knelt. With one of his gloved hands he drew the golden gun and cocked its hammer.

'I'm starting to get the feelin' that none of our plans is panning out today, old-timer!'

Tomahawk watched as two riders came galloping out of the brush to their left with their rifles blazing again. The air lit up with red shafts of hot lead. The sand started to kick up as the bullets landed all around them.

'I'd shoot back if'n I had me any damn bullets left!'

Adams aimed his gun into the shimmering heat and tried to focus on the fast-moving attackers.

Suddenly, the distant explosion of bullets that the wily old-timer had left smouldering a mile behind them in the depths of the brush filled the air. The two startled horsemen dragged on their reins as their mounts heard the small sack of bullets firing off blindly.

The old-timer got to his feet, pulled his hatchet from his belt and ran forward. With every ounce of his strength he threw it at the first stationary rider. The razor-sharp blade hit the outlaw's face dead centre. It was lethally accurate.

Before the body had rolled off the high saddle, the rancher fanned the hammer of his golden gun twice. Both his shots went through the heart of the second rider, lifting him over the saddle cantle and crashing into the sand behind his horse's hoofs.

Tomahawk ran between the riderless mounts to pluck his axe off the ground. He cleaned the blood off its honed edge across his sleeve.

'I'm startin' to think that these critters can read our minds, Gene. They knows what we're gonna do before we does.'

'How many of the varmints are left now?' Adams asked wryly before spinning the gun back into the hand-tooled holster.

'There ought to be two, I reckon, Gene,' Tomahawk replied. He examined the sheared reins hanging from his horse's bridle. 'Why?'

'That's gotta be about the right number!' said Gene Adams firmly. He turned and ran up to his horse. He leapt on to his saddle, thrust his boot-toes into the stirrups and spurred hard.

The older cowboy watched in total disbelief as his friend thundered away from him towards Alverez Falls atop his tall chestnut mare.

'Wait on up, boy!' Tomahawk vainly cried out. 'Darn ya, Gene! You're gonna get killed without me to look after ya!'

But Adams did not hear anything as he forged his way over the hot sand and up into the brush towards the trees and the falls. He was standing high in his stirrups and balancing over the neck of his chestnut mare when he saw the raging white-water ahead of him as it cascaded over the black-ened rocks and down into the mist filled lake far below.

The rancher raised his reins up to his chest and reined in hard. For a few moments he stared at the almost hypnotic water which flowed violently over the top of the falls and crashed more than a hundred feet down towards the lake. It sounded like thunder to the Bar 10 man.

The noise was deafening and yet Adams noticed

the ears of his trusty mount turn away from the river until they were aimed to something behind him.

The sound of the outlaw's Winchester being cocked drowned out everything else in Gene Adam's mind.

The rancher swung his horse around and saw the gleaming rifle in Lucifer's hands. It was aimed straight at his heart.

'So we meet again, Adams!'

'Guess this time will be the last time!' Adams drawled.

'Damn right, old man! This time I'll kill you!'

Tomahawk dragged the bridle from one of the outlaws' mounts and rushed to his own black quarter horse. His skilled hands quickly replaced the reins, then he looped them over the head and neck of the skittish creature.

'That darn fool has done gone and rushed in where the angels would be too smart to tread!' he grumbled. 'He knows that without me to save his bacon, he's not got a chance.'

The black horse turned its head and looked over the head of the bony old-timer at the sun-baked sand behind him. Tomahawk raised his eyebrows and stared at the alert animal.

'What ya seen, boy?'

The question was soon answered. Tomahawk turned and looked at the shimmering images of the twenty or more horsemen as they drove their mounts towards him. His thin hand instinctively encircled the handle of the Indian hatchet tucked in his belt as he screwed up his eyes and squinted at the approaching riders The horses were almost on top of him before his ancient eyes recognized the familiar faces of Rip Calloway and Don Miguel leading Happy Summers, Marshal Cooper and a bunch of *vaqueros* and Bar 10 cowboys.

'What in tarnation is you doing here, Rip?' Tomahawk asked when the horses were stopped next to him.

'We came to try and warn Gene that he was being tricked into riding you guys into a bush-whackin', Tomahawk!' Rip answered as he steadied his sweating mount.

'You're a tad late, son!' Tomahawk shrugged as he stepped into his stirrup and pulled himself up on to his saddle. 'We already bin bushwhacked a whole heap of times. I'm startin' to get a mite tired of it!'

'Where is Gene, Tomahawk?' Cooper asked.

'What are you doin' here, Coop?' Tomahawk asked as at last he noticed the lawman.

'Same as the rest of these boys. I'm trying to find Gene and warn him about Lucifer!' Cooper replied. 'Where is he?'

Tomahawk dragged his reins hard and turned his black horse until it was facing the falls.

'C'mon! I'll take ya there!'

Gene Adams stared down at the outlaw. He could

hardly believe the difference in the appearance of the man he had fought so furiously three years earlier. Lucifer's once handsome face was covered in brutal scars that bore testament to the power of the river rapids he had disappeared into during their last encounter.

'What's all this about, Lucifer?'

The outlaw grinned.

'I've had me a dream about this moment for so very long, Adams. A dream that just wouldn't let go. You know the sort?'

'I know the sort!' The rancher nodded. 'I've had them myself of late.'

'My dreams were about this very moment! How I'd finally have you at my mercy.'

'Revenge? Is that it?'

A sick smile etched the features of Lucifer.

'That's part of it. The rest is just plain greed. I suddenly figured out how much wealth you and García had between you. A mighty tempting reason to allow my hatred of you both to blossom. Don't you think?'

'I knew you were too smart for it to be just mindless vengeance, Lucifer. You had your sights on García's spread and the Bar 10 all the time, huh?' Adams stared hard at the man holding the rifle on him.

'Exactly.' Lucifer knew that he had only ever met one man who had bettered him. Gene Adams was that man. 'Damn! You're smart! Old, but damn smart!'

'You figuring on killing me slow?' asked Adams. He dismounted and walked closer to the rifleman. 'I reckon you must be loco if'n you think that I'll let you.'

Lucifer fired. The bullet took the hat off the rancher's head and yet Adams refused to stop approaching the outlaw.

'Stop!'

Adams smiled as he kept walking towards the man.

'Kill me if you dare, Lucifer! Or are you willing to see which of us is the faster with our guns?'

The outlaw looked confused. Again he fired. This time the bullet ripped through the left shoulder-padding of Adams's shirt.

'Stop! Listen to me, you crazy old fool!' Lucifer shouted as he found himself backing off from the smiling Bar 10 man. 'I ain't foolin' around. I'll kill you!'

Adams stopped and lowered his head until his chin touched his chest. He flexed his fingers over his gun grips.

'I'm not ready to be killed slow by an ornery critter like you, boy!' the rancher snarled. 'I intend dying fast or not at all!'

Two shots rang out and drew both men's attention.

'Take them guns out of them holsters nice and slow, old-timer.' Fern Brunnel was standing with his guns in his hands. Both barrels were smoking as the outlaw walked from the cover of the trees towards the two men. 'Why don't ya just kill him, boss? I'll do it if ya want.'

Lucifer's eyes darted at the last of his men.

'Adams is mine, Fern!'

'Reckon your boss wants to skin me alive, sonny!' The tall rancher sighed, then dropped both guns on to the dirt at his feet.

'Them guns of his are made of gold, boss,' Brunnel gasped as he found himself lured to the gleaming weapons that lay at the feet of the silent Bar 10 man. 'I never seen such guns. They must be worth a fortune.'

Lucifer walked towards Adams with the barrel of his rifle aimed at the cattle rancher's middle.

'They're yours, Fern,' the outlaw leader said. He and his last henchman closed in on the rancher.

Gene Adams did not say a word. He simply watched both men getting closer with every beat of his pounding heart.

At last they were both within spitting distance.

'He's scared, boss.' Brunnel laughed as he stooped towards the golden guns. 'Look at him sweat.'

'I know he's scared, Fern.' Lucifer smiled. He pushed the end of the rifle barrel into the middle of the rancher's stomach. 'I ought to belly-shoot him. That can take a long time to kill a critter. You wanna be belly-shot, Adams?'

Adams inhaled deeply.

'Do it!'

Suddenly the sound of a score of guns being

fired off on the prairie caught the attention of both outlaws. As their eyes darted to where they could hear the galloping riders, Adams made his move. He ripped Lucifer's rifle barrel from his hands and tossed it over the high clifftop. He then kicked out hard at the head of the outlaw as he stooped to reach for his prized guns.

The pointed cowboy boot caught Brunnel across his jaw knocking him backwards. As the stunned outlaw landed heavily on the ground, Adams pressed the gloved palm of his left hand against Lucifer's chest and swung a right uppercut. His knuckles caught him on the jaw. Lucifer went head over heels and rolled to the very edge of the wet, black rocks at the top of the waterfall.

Lucifer pushed himself up and glanced down at the sheer drop before looking at Adams again. He spat blood and then forced a laugh.

'I know women that hit harder than that, old-timer!'

Adams pulled the gloves tight over both his hands and moved above the fallen outlaw. Before he could wade in with more punches the outlaw jumped up off the ground and head-butted the rancher in the ribs.

Both men landed on the rough ground. Adams felt the back of his head crack against a jagged stone and screwed his eyes up in agony. He did not see any of the half-dozen blows that rained into his face and chest.

Then he felt the hands of the outlaw grabbing

his collar and dragging him upright. He shook his head and managed to clear his mind long enough to focus his eyes on his opponent.

He smashed two hard jabs into the belly of the outlaw and could feel the wind being knocked out of him. He pushed Lucifer backwards and then crossed a perfectly timed right on to the point of the younger man's chin.

Lucifer staggered backwards to the very rim of the high waterfall. Water vapour sprayed over him and cleared the outlaw's head just in time. He stopped and looked over his shoulder down into the lake far below.

'Good, but not good enough!' he said defiantly as blood dripped from his broken teeth.

Adams started after the outlaw and then noticed the man drawing a gun from inside his jacket. The outlaw steadied himself and then cocked its hammer.

The rancher's hands went for his holsters.

Suddenly Adams realized that his own matched pair of golden guns were still on the ground behind him. His head turned and looked at the guns that had found themselves in the hands of the dazed Brunnel who was rising to his feet. He returned his attention to the smiling Lucifer and shook his head.

'Looks like you got the drop on me this time, boys!' Adams admitted.

'Let me shoot him, boss!' Brunnel growled.

Lucifer raised his own gun and aimed it at Adams's head.

147

'I told ya! He's mine!'

Then the deafening sound of guns being fired again drew all three men's attention as twenty riders came up through the trees towards them. Adams could not believe his eyes when he saw Tomahawk leading Marshal Cooper, Don Miguel as well as *vaqueros* and many of his Bar 10 cowboys.

'Looks like my boys have come visiting, Lucifer.'

The outlaw leader's face went grim as he took another backward step closer to the edge of the high waterfall.

'I'll kill you if they open up with them guns, Adams!'

Brunnel had managed to get back to his feet and was about to fire the golden guns when half a dozen shots tore through the air and cut him down. The riders all drew in their horses and stopped when they saw the gun trained on Gene Adams.

'What'll we do, Gene?' Rip Calloway shouted out.

Adams stared at Lucifer and the gun which was aimed at him.

'Stay where you are, boys! I'll handle this!'

Lucifer could no longer control his rage. He went to take a step towards the calm rancher when his left foot slipped from under him on the damp rocks. As he stumbled, his gun fired sending a bullet within an inch of Gene Adams. Then, as if from nowhere, the chilling sound of the deadly tomahawk filled the ears of both men who faced one another as it flew through the air.

Adams watched as the Indian axe bounced off the face of the outlaw. The force of the impact sent Lucifer reeling on his heels. Then both his boots slipped from under him and he tumbled backwards. A last wild shot came from the barrel of the gun again and then he fell.

Every eye watched in a mixture of horror and satisfaction as Lucifer went over the top of the falls. Adams ran to the edge of the high waterfall. His eyes narrowed when he saw the outlaw's body crash over one jagged rock after another as it plummeted down into the raging white-water spray before disappearing into the mist.

Tomahawk moved cautiously to the rancher's side.

'That's how to kill a critter, Gene!'

Adams watched the older man pick up his tomahawk and walk back to the rest of the riders.

'You saved my bacon,' Adams said, walking to where his guns lay. He plucked them up and slid them into his holsters.

'Again,' Tomahawk added.

Gene Adams looked at his men in disbelief.

'What you boys doing here?'

Happy removed his hat.

'There was a few more of us to start with, Gene. We lost a few boys back on Smoky Mountain.'

'We came to warn you, Gene,' Cooper said.

'You need faster horses.' Adams rubbed the blood from the corner of his mouth and then

looked into the face of Don Miguel García.
Both men nodded to one another.
There were no more words.

FINALE

The courtyard within the mansion of the García family was bathed in the warming sun of another new day. It seemed that all the horror which had gone before it was nothing more than a bad dream. A nightmare that the proud men who were gathered around the noble Mexican had to try and come to terms with. None of them had ever experienced anything quite so brutal before and they knew that if they were lucky, they might never be forced to endure anything like it again. They had all suffered at the hands of the strange outlaw known as Lucifer and his hired gunmen. Yet they were still defiant. It took a lot more than bullets to frighten the riders of the Bar 10.

Gene Adams ran his gloved hand along the neck of his chestnut mare and studied those who were left of his cowboys. He handed the reins to Happy Summers and then turned to Don Miguel García

151

and lowered his head as he gripped the brim of his ten-gallon hat.

'Luis was a fine man, Don Miguel. He deserved better than to fall foul of that evil outlaw.'

The Mexican sighed and raised his head.

'*Sí, amigo.* He was a great man. I was always proud of him and shall remain so until my dying day. But you and your friends are the same as Luis. You are brave. The way you have helped my people and me, shall never be forgotten.'

'All we did was fight, Don Miguel,' Adams said modestly.

García patted the Texan's shoulder.

'No, Señor Gene. You did much more than just fight. You and your Bar 10 cowboys risked everything to save the lives of all who dwell in my hacienda. You are men. Real men.'

'What will you do now?' Adams asked.

'I still have my horses, *amigo.*' García nodded as he stared down at the handsome palomino horses who were looking over the doors of their stalls. 'I still have my horses.'

Adams watched Tomahawk amble up beside him and then shook the hand of the elegant Mexican who strolled toward his beloved horses.

'That's a very fine man, old-timer.'

'Yep. He sure is, Gene,' Tomahawk agreed. 'A fine man with a broken heart.'

The two men walked into the cool interior of the house and along the tiled hall until they reached the guest room. Adams knocked and then led the way in. The smiling face of Johnny greeted them.

'He looks a lot better, Gene.'

'At least one of us does, Tomahawk.' Johnny grinned.

'I was out there fighting outlaws, boy.' The old cowboy sniffed. 'Risking my life whilst you was here sleeping.'

'He was unconscious, Tomahawk,' Gene Adams corrected.

'What's that mean?'

'It means, he was asleep.'

Tomahawk gave a toothless grin.

'See?'

Gene Adams ran a gloved hand over Johnny Puma's hair and then looked to Tomahawk.

'Reckon this puppy ought to be fit to ride in a couple of weeks' time, old-timer?'

'Well, I ain't too sure, Gene,' Tomahawk replied as both his bushy eyebrows sought and found the upturned brim of his battered hat. 'He still looks a mite sickly to me.'

Adams grinned.

'He always looks sickly.'

'Darn tootin', boy. Darn tootin'.' Tomahawk laughed out loud as he slapped his skinny hip.

Johnny eased himself up in the large soft bed and stared at his pals. He was still weak from his ordeal but eager to join his friends on the long ride home to the Bar 10.

'I'm OK, boys,' he insisted. 'Honest. Don't go

leavin' me here all on my lonesome. I'm fit enough to ride back home.'

Gene Adams sat on the bed and looked into the young face.

'No you ain't. Anyway, I ain't leaving you on your own, Johnny. I'm leaving old Tomahawk here with you. When you're all mended, you can both ride back to the ranch.'

Johnny's eyes darted to Tomahawk's toothless grin.

'You're leaving me here with him? That's darn cruel.'

Tomahawk's expression changed.

'What's wrong with me staying to look after ya?'

'You ain't no company, old-timer.' Johnny sighed. 'You'll be moanin' and groanin' all the time.'

Tomahawk wrinkled up his nose.

'Why, you young whippersnapper. I ought to tan your hide.'

Adams raised his hands as if declaring a truce between the two men.

'Easy, boys. It'll not be so bad. You can rest up and take in this nice Mexican air, Johnny.' The rancher sighed. 'And Tomahawk, you can rest your bones. Drink plenty of Don Miguel's wine and relax. You deserve it.'

Both cowboys stared at one another, then their faces lit up and they both chuckled.

'I'm only joshin', Gene. Reckon a man couldn't find a better companion than Tomahawk.' Johnny rested his head against the white pillows and looked around the well-furnished room. It was the first time that he had really seen it since he'd woken up after his operation. 'Say, this is better than our ranch house. A man could enjoy being sick here.'

Adams glanced around the room and nodded.

'A tad fancy, but OK.'

Suddenly the door of the guest room opened wider and a slim young female walked in with a jug of water in her hands. She was beautiful and all three men noticed.

'I bring you some water, Señor Johnny,' she said as she rested the jug on the dresser next to the bed.

Johnny's eyes widened. He went to raise his head off the pillow but her small hand rested on his temple and pushed him gently back.

'Who are you, ma'am?' Johnny asked.

'I am Rosita. My mother is the cook,' she replied as she stroked his brow. 'Don Miguel has told me that I am to look after you until you are well again.'

'Gosh.' Johnny gasped as her soft hand stroked his temple. 'That's just fine, Rosita.'

'Anything you want, I am to give to you,' Rosita said. Her long, dark eyelashes fluttered. 'I have been ordered by Don Miguel to make sure you want for nothing.'

'Gosh!' Johnny repeated.

Tomahawk eased himself next to Adams and whispered:

'I got me a feelin' that Johnny here is gonna take the longest time to recover, Gene. Mind you, if I was in his place, I think I'd not be in no hurry either.'

Adams smiled and tugged at his pal's jutting beard.

'I'm leaving you here to look after him. I don't want you getting into any trouble. Understand?'

There was a twinkle in Tomahawk's ancient eyes.

'You can trust me, Gene.'

Adams's head nodded slowly up and down.

'Sure I can.'

Rosita moved around the bed and then headed for the open doorway. She paused when Tomahawk winked at her.

'You are a very naughty old man, I think.'

'Darn tootin'!' Tomahawk agreed.

The well-built cook entered the room and stood beside her daughter. She smiled at all three men. Her attention was then drawn to the skinny Tomahawk. She blushed and moved closer to him.

She touched his beard, then giggled.

'I like a man with a beard, Señor Tomahawk. All three of my husbands had beards. I find them so very attractive. The sign of a real man.'

Tomahawk gulped and blinked hard. He then clapped his bony hands together in excitement.

'I'm darn covered in hair, ya know? I even got hair I ain't ever used yet.'

'I will see you later, *señor*.' The cook smiled and walked out from the room.

156

'I think I'm gonna like stayin' down here in ol' Mexico, Gene.' Tomahawk said.

Adams grinned.

'She's already buried three husbands, old-timer. I'd be careful if I was you.'

'I ain't afraid. A man has to take a few risks.'

'You just remember that I'm the one who needs nursin' back to health, Tomahawk!' Johnny laughed.

'That boy is just plumb selfish, Gene!' Tomahawk winked.

Gene Adams eased himself up off the bed, placed his hat on over his white hair and tightened the drawstring until it was under his chin.

'Well I reckon I better get going, boys. Happy and Rip and the rest of the boys are waiting out in the courtyard.'

Johnny grabbed the rancher's gloved hand and looked Gene Adams in the eye.

'Thanks, Gene.'

'For what, Johnny? Leaving you here with this old fossil or leaving you here with such a pretty nurse?'

Johnny's face was serious.

'Don Miguel told me what you done for me, Gene. I'd have died if'n you hadn't been willing to save me. I'm grateful.'

Adams patted the cowboy's hair and smiled wide and long.

'Gratitude ain't needed, son. A man looks after his family the best he can. I was never blessed with any real sons, so I gotta take care of you boys.'

'I'm still grateful.' Johnny watched the tall man head towards the door.

Gene Adams rested a hand on the dark-stained wooden door and then looked over his broad shoulder at the handsome cowboy.

'I owed you, Johnny. That bullet ought to have hit Tomahawk or me, but you pushed us out of the way. You took lead for us and that shows that you're a man, Johnny. A real man.'

'A Bar 10 man, Gene?'

Adams glanced at Tomahawk, then they both looked straight at their injured friend propped up against the mountain of soft pillows.

'Ya darn tootin', Johnny!' They both smiled. 'Darn tootin', you are!'